Jack knows every wrestling move there is to know, and his dreams come true when he's recruited as a training assistant to Waldo's Wrestling Trolls.
But Jack has a secret that even he doesn't know, which will let him actually join the trolls in the ring!

JIM ELDRIDGE

WRESTLING TROLLS

MATCH 1

BIG ROCK and the MASKED AVENGER

Illustrated by JAN BIELECKI

HOT
KEY
BOOKS

First published in Great Britain in 2014 by Hot Key Books
Northburgh House, 10 Northburgh Street, London EC1V 0AT

Text copyright © Jim Eldridge 2014

A CIP catalogue record for this book is available from the British Library.

ISBN Paperback edition: 978-1-4714-0193-0
ISBN Library edition: 978-1-4714-0392-7

1

This book is typeset in 11pt Sabon using Atomik ePublisher

Printed and bound by Clays Ltd, St Ives Plc

FSC

Hot Key Books supports the Forest Stewardship Council (FSC),
the leading international forest certification organisation, and is committed to
printing only on Greenpeace-approved FSC-certified paper.

www.hotkeybooks.com

Hot Key Books is part of the Bonnier Publishing Group
www.bonnierpublishing.com

*From Big Rock to his own
Princess Ava and Jack*

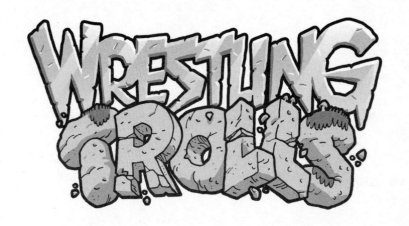

Contents

WALDO'S WRESTLING TROLLS

Chapter 1

The Master of Ceremonies stood in the centre of the wrestling ring, the spangles on his shiny multicoloured suit reflecting the glare from the lighting rigs high up in the ceiling of the enormous tent.

'My lords, ladies and gentlemen!' his voice boomed out. 'Welcome to the second fantastic day of this very special All-Comers Slamdown, being held in the grounds of the magnificent Veto Castle. Once again I give you: Orcs versus Trolls!'

At this a huge roar of appreciation came from the audience. Even though it was the first bout of the day and early in the morning, the tent was packed. People stood on their seats and shouted, some waved homemade signs and pictures declaring their admiration for their favourite wrestlers, while others chanted and sang.

'Orcs! Orcs! Orcs!' came the chant from one side of the audience, while another equally large group sang loudly, and in chorus: 'Trolls! Trolls! Trolls!'

The MC beamed happily as the shouting from all around the tent grew to a crescendo, before he waved a hand to calm the crowd down and announced:

'Today it gives me great pleasure to introduce you to the very special patron for this wrestling tournament, someone whose family has long been involved in the noble art of wrestling. My lords, ladies and gentlemen, please show your appreciation for our very special guest, from the Royal Court of the Kingdom of Weevil: Her Royal Highness Princess Ava!'

Once more the crowd erupted into loud cheers and placard waving, and this time the chants were of, 'Ava! Ava! Ava!'

Outside the tent, in the grey morning as the rain battered down, ten-year-old Jack balanced on a wobbly box as he peered through a gap in the tent. In the royal box he could see a small girl standing up and waving at the crowd. She wore an ornately embroidered dress of purple and blue, and had a small gold crown on top of her wavy red hair.

That's so unfair, Jack thought miserably. I bet she doesn't know a quarter as much as I do about wrestling, but there she is in the best seat in the house. Why can't I get a good seat in the dry,

instead of being out here, soaking wet and balancing on this box?

It had been raining heavily for the last hour and Jack was soaked right through to the skin. He looked through the hole in the tent and saw the crowd settle back down in their seats and fall silent in an expectant hush as the MC strode around the ring, smiling broadly.

'The first bout on this final day is between that fantastic Wrestling Troll, Mudd . . .'

Before the MC could finish the sentence, at the word 'Mudd' half of the huge crowd erupted into cheers and yells and chants of, 'Mudd! Mudd!' and placards with a picture of a ball of mud on them were waved. Meanwhile, from the other half of the audience came loud jeers and boos.

From his vantage point, Jack saw the figure of Mudd enter the tent from a door at the back. The troll was huge and wearing a sparkly blue and yellow costume. He was also well-named – over his rock-like body he seemed to have a coating of wet mud, which would make it difficult for his opponent to get a decent hold.

The tall, powerful figure of Mudd stomped down the aisle towards the ring, waving at the crowd who stood and cheered – or stood and booed if they were orc supporters.

Mudd reached the ring and hauled himself up between the ropes, then stamped around waving at the crowd before stopping at his corner, flexing his arm muscles and bending his knees in a warm-up.

The MC continued: '. . . and one of the rising stars from Lord Veto's stable of sporting heroes, Wrestling Orc . . . Slasher!'

At this, the section of the crowd that had been booing Mudd suddenly began roaring their approval of Slasher the Wrestling Orc, and now the placards that were being waved had a picture of a sharp claw and the word 'Slasher' on them, along with chants of, 'Slasher! Slasher!' and 'Orcs! Orcs! Orcs!'

Where the troll had marched in a flat-footed, heavy way down the aisle, Slasher the Orc ran out from the door at the far end, did a dazzling somersault and then leapt to his feet, baring his large teeth in a wicked grin and holding his claws so that the light reflected from his shiny talons. He wore shorts, which meant that his scaly skin was on show for all to see.

As Slasher danced down the aisle towards the ring, Jack turned his attention back to Mudd the Troll, standing patiently as he waited for his opponent to get into the ring. It was the Wrestling Trolls Jack had really come to see. The problem was that now the wrestlers had appeared, some people at the back of the crowd were standing up and blocking Jack's view through the hole in the tent.

He saw another hole a bit to the left, and shifted to try and reach it, while holding onto the fabric of the tent; but just as he moved, an angry growl from behind startled him, and he fell off the box onto the wet ground.

Jack struggled to his feet and turned to find himself looking into the angry face of the owner of Veto Castle, Lord Veto himself! Next to Lord Veto stood the tall, powerful figure of Warg, one of his Wrestling Orcs.

'So!' snarled Lord Veto. 'My kitchen boy! What are you doing here?'

'I . . . er . . . I . . .' stammered Jack. He gulped nervously, then said apologetically: 'I'm sorry, my Lord.'

'You will be sorry!' snapped Lord Veto. 'You're sacked! And if you dare to come anywhere near my castle again, you'll suffer!'

Jack stared up at Lord Veto, shocked.

'But . . . but I only wanted to see the wrestling, my Lord!' he said.

'And I forbade you to! You disobeyed me! Warg, find a big muddy puddle and throw him into it!'

The huge orc standing beside Lord Veto growled. Then it reached out one of its massive claws and grabbed Jack, and carried him off into the rainy night. Jack struggled, trying to break free, and for a second a kind of mist filled Jack's mind and he seemed to see everything through crystals. A shuddering sensation pumped through his arms and legs, and the orc nearly dropped him. Then the strange feelings vanished and the orc tightened its grip on Jack and carried him across the muddy field, while the rain poured down. Finally the orc stopped and, with a satisfied laugh, dropped Jack into a large muddy puddle. Then it returned to Lord Veto and the two walked towards the entrance of the large tent.

Chapter 2

Jack got up out of the puddle, and then fell over as his feet slipped on the mud. He lay there, half in and half out of the big puddle, and felt the rain fall on him. He thought he might be crying, but his face was so wet from the rain that he couldn't be sure if there were also tears.

'Hello! What's up?'

Jack looked up at the sound of the deep friendly voice. A troll was standing there, looking down at him sympathetically. The troll was wearing its wrestling costume: a multicoloured leotard with a picture of a mountaintop on the front. Up close like this, Jack noticed that the mixture of colours was a mostly to do with the fact that the costume had been patched with lots of different coloured cloth: blue, red, yellow, green, purple.

'An orc dumped me in this puddle,' said Jack. And now he *was* crying. 'A Wrestling Orc.'

'Orcs no good,' said the troll, and he made a fart noise just to make its feelings about orcs clear. 'I take you somewhere dry. Make you feel better.'

'Thanks,' said Jack, 'but there's no need.'

The troll made the fart noise again and lifted Jack up as if he weighed no more than a feather. Then it carried him through the squelching mud to a large wooden caravan. The troll pushed open the door.

'Milo!' it called. 'We got visitor!'

A boy of about thirteen looked up from his wrestling magazine as the troll pushed the soaking wet Jack into the caravan.

'Found him in puddle,' explained the troll. 'He wet.'

'So I see,' said the boy. He put down the magazine and stood up, smiling in greeting. 'Let me guess! You want some signed photographs of Big Rock?' Milo went to a drawer and opened it, taking out some large glossy photos as he carried on talking: 'Or maybe you want a piece of his costume? That is our most popular item! That's why his costume's got so many patches on it – because of all the people who want a bit, just so they can say that they own a genuine piece of Big Rock the Wrestling Troll!'

'He not buying,' said the troll. 'He sad. And wet.'

'Not buying?' said Milo, shocked. 'Everyone buys!'

'Not me,' said Jack sadly. 'I haven't got any money.'

This admission made Milo stop.

'None?' he queried, puzzled, as if the thought of people without any money at all was an alien concept for him.

'None,' sighed Jack.

Milo looked at Jack, and now properly took in his soaking wet, mud-stained clothes.

'What's your name?' asked Milo.

'Jack,' said Jack.

'I'm Milo, and that's Big Rock,' said Milo. 'He's the Champion Wrestling Troll.'

'Not yet,' said Big Rock in his deep troll voice.

'The next Champion Wrestling Troll,' said Milo. 'I'm his manager and trainer. So, how did you end up in a puddle?'

'Lord Veto told one of his orcs to dump me in it.'

Milo looked interested.

'Lord Veto? The bloke who owns all those sports stars? Wrestling Orcs? Footballing Elves? Gymnast Goblins?'

'Yes,' said Jack. 'I work – worked – in the kitchens at Veto Castle. I've worked there since I was five. Until tonight. He sacked me.'

And Jack told them his story. Orphaned at five years old. His parents had worked for Lord Veto, so Jack was kept on to work in the kitchens at Veto Castle, doing all the dirty jobs that no one else wanted to do, like cleaning the grease from under the oven. But Jack's biggest love was wrestling, and when he'd heard that a tournament featuring Wrestling Trolls was to be held in the grounds of Veto Castle, he'd asked Lord Veto if he could have a day off to go and watch it.

The answer had been a firm refusal.

'He said no, I had to stay in the kitchens in case he felt like a snack when he came home. So all day long yesterday I stayed in the kitchen, but he never came. So today I thought I'd be able to go without him noticing. So I did.'

'Then you saw the first match!' smiled Milo. 'Slasher versus Mudd! Fantastic!'

'I never saw it,' Jack told them miserably. 'I never got in. I had a penny saved up from my wages, but I lost it through a hole in my pocket. So I found a gap in the tent I could look through, but I couldn't see properly. I was just getting a decent view when Lord Veto found me. And that was that. He sacked me and had me dumped in the puddle.'

Milo shook his head. 'I think that's one of the saddest stories I've ever heard,' he said. He turned to Big Rock. 'What do you think?'

'Sad,' agreed the troll, nodding his great rock-like head.

'No, I mean: what do you think we should do with him?' said Milo.

Big Rock fell silent. A minute passed. Then another.

'He's thinking,' Milo explained to Jack. 'Trolls aren't used to doing too much of that.' He turned back to Big Rock. 'Well?'

The huge troll finally nodded. 'Help Jack,' he said.

'Yes. That's what I thought,' nodded Milo. He turned to Jack. 'I've got some old clothes you can put on. They may be a bit big for you, but at least you'll be dry while we hang out those wet ones of yours. Then you can give me and Big Rock a hand, practising for his bout this afternoon. If it stops raining, that is.'

Big Rock lifted his head and listened.

'It stop,' he said.

'What?' asked Milo.

He went to the window and looked out, and then he smiled.

'You're right, Big Rock. It has stopped raining,' he said. He grinned at Jack. 'Maybe you're bringing us luck!'

Chapter 3

As the grass was still wet, Milo had spread a tarpaulin on the ground so that he and Big Rock wouldn't get soaked as they practised wrestling moves. Jack sat on the steps of the caravan and watched the pair. He was wearing an old shirt and trousers of Milo's, which were so big on him he'd had to tie a length of string round the waist to stop the clothes falling off.

Big Rock and Milo had gone through different throws and holds – in all of which, Jack noticed, Big Rock was very gentle with the way he handled Milo, always catching him with one of his enormous rocky hands before Milo hit the tarpaulin.

Jack felt a huge thrill at the realisation that

he was enjoying his own private show, watching a real Wrestling Troll up close!

Milo got up from a fall and faced Big Rock.

'Put both your arms around the back of my head,' said Milo. As the huge troll gently did this, Milo added: 'Good. That's a Collar Tie.'

'No it isn't,' said Jack.

Milo and Big Rock turned to Jack.

'What?' said Milo.

Milo looked annoyed, and Jack cursed himself silently for blurting out what he'd just said, but it had been an automatic reaction. He wondered whether to just apologise and keep quiet, but he couldn't. Jack loved wrestling and he'd read everything he could get his hands on about the sport. He knew that the hold Milo had just described wasn't a Collar Tie.

'That's a Tie Clinch,' said Jack. 'A Collar Tie is when he's got just his hands on the back of your neck. When his arms are around the back of your head, that's a Tie Clinch.'

'Rubbish!' snorted Milo.

'Er . . .' said the troll thoughtfully.

Milo looked at Big Rock. 'What?' he asked.

'Jack right,' said Big Rock. 'It Tie Clinch. I remember.'

'Rubbish!' snorted Milo again.

'It is,' said Big Rock. 'Waldo tell me.'

'Who's Waldo?' asked Jack.

Milo pointed to the large letters WWT painted on the side of the caravan in faded colours.

'WWT. Waldo's Wrestling Trolls. My uncle Waldo. He used to run this travelling wrestling show.'

'Lots of trolls then,' nodded Big Rock. 'Ten Wrestling Trolls.'

'Wow!' said Jack, awed. 'What happened to them?'

'Uncle Waldo retired, and he asked me if I'd like to take it over. I'd been helping him, so I said yes. As for the Wrestling Trolls, most of them decided to retire at the same time. So that just left me, and Big Rock.'

'Tie Clinch,' said Big Rock. 'Waldo tell me.'

'You're both wrong,' said Milo firmly. 'And I'll prove it. I've got a book inside with every

32

wrestling hold there is. I shall prove that's a Collar Tie.'

With that, Milo went back inside the caravan.

Jack looked at Big Rock. 'Have you been wrestling a long time?'

'Long time,' said Big Rock, nodding. 'Good fun. Except against orcs. Orcs cheat.'

'Yes,' said Jack sadly. 'Orcs are horrible.'

Milo returned. He looked thoughtful.

'All right,' he said. 'You've passed the test.'

'What test?' asked Jack.

'I was just testing you to see if you knew about the different wrestling holds. That's why I said that was a Collar Tie instead of a Tie Clinch, to see if you'd correct me.'

Big Rock chuckled, a low rumbling sound.

'Milo got it wrong,' he grinned.

'No I didn't,' said Milo defensively. 'I did it on purpose. I always knew it was really a Tie Clinch. I just wanted to see if Jack here knew what it was.'

'Tie Clinch,' nodded Big Rock. 'Jack right.'

'Exactly,' said Milo. 'But I wanted to check

before I offered him the job.'

Jack looked at Milo, hope flickering in his heart. A job!

'What job?' he asked.

'Joining us,' said Milo. 'Me and Big Rock. You can be the assistant trainer.'

'Me?'

'Well, you obviously know a bit about wrestling. And you can help look after Robin.'

Jack looked around, puzzled. Who was Robin?

'Who's Robin?' he asked aloud.

'He is,' said Milo, pointing.

Jack followed Milo's finger, and saw a shaggy-looking horse grazing on the grass and looking at him.

'I am,' said the horse.

'He doesn't wrestle as well, does he?' asked Jack.

Milo and Big Rock laughed. The horse, Robin, didn't join in the laughter.

'The boy's an idiot,' said the horse grumpily.

'Robin pulls the caravan,' said Milo.

'Yes, I can help look after a horse!' said Jack, his face breaking into a huge smile.

'Great!' said Milo. 'Welcome to the Big Rock Travelling Wrestling Show!'

Chapter 4

Jack spent the next hour watching Milo and Big Rock train, now and then suggesting they try a particular hold, or a throw.

'Try a Bulldog!' Jack cried, or, 'Give him a Giant Swing!'

And Big Rock and Milo would go through that particular move.

I'm so happy, thought Jack. I'm training with a real wrestler! A Wrestling Troll!

Jack's biggest moment of happiness came when he called out: 'Do a Mountain Bomb!' and Milo turned to him and asked, 'What's a Mountain Bomb?'

I know something they don't! thought Jack delightedly.

Jack began to explain, going through the actions with the huge troll. 'The wrestler lets the opponent rush towards him. Then the wrestler ducks and hooks one of the opponent's legs with his arm . . . Like so!' And Jack ducked down and put his forearm against one of Big Rock's massive legs. 'Then the wrestler stands up and falls backwards, flipping the opponent and driving him back-first down to the mat, and then lands on the opponent. A Mountain Bomb will be a perfect move for Big Rock, because he's got a picture of a mountain on his costume.'

'Brilliant!' said Milo. 'Give it a try, Big Rock!'

Big Rock did a backwards fall and flipped Jack into the air. For an awful moment, Jack thought he was going to land heavily and hurt himself, but then one of Big Rock's enormous hands shot out and grabbed Jack safely and gently, and put him down.

'Good move!' grunted Big Rock, getting to his feet.

Jack smiled broadly. He'd never felt so happy in his life.

'Okay,' said Milo. 'Lunch break!'

'I'll cook it!' said Jack.

'You?' asked Milo.

'Yes,' said Jack. 'I was a kitchen boy at Lord Veto's castle, remember. I know all about cooking!'

'Yes, well, in our case there's not much cooking involved,' said Milo. 'Big Rock eats rocks, and Robin eats grass. So there's usually only me, and I just have a sandwich or something.'

'Not today!' exclaimed Jack. 'Today I'm going to cook you something special!'

Milo and Big Rock carried on training while Jack was away foraging, and a short while later Jack returned, the basket filled with a mixture of greenery and vegetables.

'Lunch in half an hour,' said Jack, and he disappeared into the caravan.

'Okay, Big Rock,' said Milo. 'You might as well have yours.'

Big Rock sat down on the ground and opened

up a small sack, and took some rocks and stones out of it. They were all different sorts and different sizes: small pebbles, chunks of granite and quartz, and some soft pieces of clay.

Big Rock picked out a small round smoky-black pebble and looked at it fondly.

'Quartz!' he said happily. 'Taste best!'

And he popped it into his mouth.

Robin was already grazing on the long, sweet grass. Milo sat next to Big Rock munching on his rocks and pebbles and thought to himself: I should have just stuck to a cheese sandwich. Then the smells started to waft out from the caravan, smells that smelt . . . wonderful. His stomach rumbled. And then Jack appeared down the steps of the caravan, holding a tray with two wooden soup bowls, along with some bread. He gave one of the bowls to Milo.

'Here,' he said.

As Milo and Jack tucked into the soup, they were aware of Robin appearing beside them.

'What's that?' asked the horse, lifting its nose in the air and sniffing.

'Would you like some?' asked Jack.

'No,' said Milo, between mouthfuls. 'Horses only eat grass and oats.'

'Usually,' said Robin sharply, with a glare at Milo. 'But, maybe, just to show goodwill, I might try a sip.'

'No problem,' said Jack. 'There's some left in the pan.'

And he hurried into the caravan, and came out a moment later with a large bowl of soup, which he put down on the grass in front of the horse.

'There!' he said.

Robin put his nose down and sniffed at the bowl, and then tentatively put out his tongue and stuck it into the mixture. There were a few light slurping sounds, and then one mighty slurp and the contents of the bowl disappeared into Robin's mouth.

As Jack picked up the empty bowls and took them into the caravan, Milo grinned at Robin.

'Well?' he asked.

The horse gave a grunt. 'He can cook. I'll give him that.'

Chapter 5

After lunch, when everything had been cleared away, Jack asked, 'What happens now?'

'Now we get ready for Big Rock's bout this afternoon to decide who gets to go up against Aggro in the exhibition match tonight.'

Aggro! thought Jack excitedly. One of Lord Veto's Wrestling Orcs. Jack had sometimes seen Aggro at a distance, practising throws, but had never been allowed near him. No one except Lord Veto and his trainer were allowed near Aggro. Aggro was special. Aggro was the National Wrestling Champion!

Milo pulled out a large watch and looked at it.

'In fact, we'd better go and get Big Rock registered.'

'Big Rock already register,' grunted the troll.

'That was just for yesterday's bout,' said Milo. 'We've got to register you again for the match against Mudd.'

'Mudd?' said Jack. 'He was the one I saw . . . well, started to see . . . this morning. He was up against Slasher the Orc.'

'And he beat him,' smiled Milo.

'Mudd good Wrestling Troll,' said Big Rock.

'He's also a very slippery customer,' said Milo. 'It won't be an easy contest.' He turned to Jack and asked him: 'Would you go with Big Rock and register him for today's bout?'

Jack was the proudest he'd ever felt as he and Big Rock entered the tent and walked up to the registration desk. The enormous figure of Mudd was already at the desk, with a small dwarf beside him, who was filling in the forms. Jack and Big Rock took their place behind Mudd and waited, and a feeling of excitement filled Jack. And then Jack heard a harsh voice snarl behind them.

'You!' barked Lord Veto. 'Kitchen boy!'

Big Rock turned and glowered at Lord Veto. 'His name Jack,' grunted Big Rock.

'I don't care what his name is,' snapped Lord Veto. He turned on Jack and snarled: 'I told you never to come back on my property again, or you'd suffer. Well, suffer is what you're going to do!' With that, he called out: 'Warg!'

As the large orc ambled towards them, a nasty smile on its face and flexing its claws, Jack thought about running away. But then he thought: no! I have a right to be here!

He was surprised to hear himself saying the words aloud: 'No! I have a right to be here!'

Lord Veto stared at Jack, stunned. 'What did you say?' he demanded.

'I have a right to be here,' repeated Jack. 'I'm registering my wrestler.' And he indicated Big Rock.

Lord Veto looked at the massive figure of Big Rock, and then back at Jack again, still stunned. Warg the Orc had stopped approaching and was watching the scene, aware that something odd was happening, but not sure what.

'Your wrestler?' echoed Lord Veto.

'I'm his assistant trainer,' nodded Jack.

'He is,' said Big Rock, in a deep rumbling voice.

A small, smartly dressed dwarf appeared.

'Is there a problem, Lord Veto?' he asked. 'I'm Alexander Hobnob from the Wrestling Federation.'

'There certainly is!' snapped Lord Veto. He pointed an angry finger at Jack. 'I banned this boy from ever coming onto my land again, but here he is claiming to be the trainer of this

Wrestling Troll.'

'Assistant trainer,' corrected Jack. He turned to the dwarf and said: 'This is Big Rock.'

'Yes, I know of Big Rock, I've seen him wrestle many times,' said the dwarf. To Big Rock he asked: 'And is this young person your assistant trainer?'

'Yes,' said Big Rock.

'In that case, Lord Veto, the boy is perfectly entitled to be here.'

'But this is my land!' burst out Lord Veto. 'My grounds! My castle!'

'And you have hired them out for the occasion to the Wrestling Federation, so our rules apply,' said Alexander Hobnob. He turned to the clerk sitting behind the registration desk. 'Please register this young man and the troll.'

With that, he turned and trotted off.

Lord Veto glared at Jack. His face had gone red and his ears were almost purple with rage. Jack was worried that he might actually burst.

'This isn't over, kitchen boy!' he snarled. 'I'll have my own back on you, see if I don't!'

Chapter 6

Lord Veto stomped angrily out of the tent, almost knocking Milo over as the young wrestling manager came in. Milo looked after the departing Lord Veto, then turned to Jack and Big Rock.

'Any trouble?' he asked.

Jack hesitated. He was about to tell Milo about the threats from Lord Veto, but then he thought, no. That problem was solved. They had more important things to think about: the match.

'No,' he said.

'Good,' said Milo. 'Let's go and get ready.'

Jack followed Big Rock and Milo down a corridor to a small room off the main tent.

'This is where we wait until Big Rock's name is called,' said Milo.

The loudspeaker on the wall hummed into life, and Jack could hear the sound of cheering and shouting, and not just from the loudspeaker – it could be heard coming through to them from the arena inside the main tent.

'My lords, ladies and gentlemen!' came the voice of the Master of Ceremonies. 'Next on the bill, the battle for a place in the final of the All-Comers Slamdown, with the chance for the winner to take on one of the greatest wrestlers of all time, the National Wrestling Champion, Aggro the fantastic orc, in an exhibition match!'

At this there was a massive cheer from the audience and chants of, 'Orcs! Orcs! Orcs!'

'This is it,' muttered Milo. 'You ready, Big Rock?'

'I ready,' nodded the troll.

'So, my lords, ladies and gentlemen!' they heard the MC say in ringing tones. 'Please welcome to the arena, that incredible Wrestling Troll . . . Mudd!'

Mudd had obviously entered the arena, because the audience went wild with more shouting and cheering and yells and screaming chants of, 'Mudd! Mudd!'

Jack could imagine the scene outside, the placards being waved, the crowd on their feet, their fists pumping into the air, many wearing the different costumes of their favourites, some with their faces painted in the colours of their favoured wrestler.

'Ready, Jack?' asked Milo.

'Ready,' nodded Jack. And then he suddenly realised with a shock that he didn't know what he had to do when they got out there. 'What do I do?' he asked, horrified.

'Just be there in the corner with us,' said Milo. 'Watch out for any fouls from the opponent. Though that doesn't usually happen with Wrestling Trolls.'

'Mudd good wrestler,' nodded Big Rock. 'Fight fair.'

As the cheering from the arena died down, from the loudspeaker they heard the MC declaim: 'And now, please welcome, Mudd's opponent, the truly formidable troll . . . Big Rock!'

Again, the roar of the crowd rose, and as Milo flung open the tent flap for them to enter the arena, the sound was almost deafening.

Milo led the way, Big Rock following, with Jack marching proudly behind them down the aisle as they made their way to the wrestling ring.

The placards being waved excitedly as they marched down the aisle had pictures of a mountaintop on them, the same image that was on Big Rock's multicoloured costume. The crowd were going wild, many reaching out to try and touch Big Rock as they passed.

'Rock! Rock! Rock!' they sang. 'Big Rock!'

As they passed the royal box, Jack saw the small figure of Princess Ava had stood up from the ornate golden chair provided for her, and he noticed that even she was smiling and clapping her hands as Big Rock passed her on his way down the aisle.

They reached the ring and Big Rock hauled himself up between the ropes and clambered in. Jack was about to climb up after him, but Milo grabbed him and pulled him back down.

'We stay here,' he hissed, and he indicated two stools in the corner, below the edge of the ring.

Jack was too excited to sit down. He looked up into the ring, where the referee was reminding the crowd of the rules.

'The winner is the first to get two pinfalls, two submissions, or a knockout!' boomed the referee.

Pinfalls, nodded Jack. Holding your opponent down with both shoulders touching the mat, for a count of three. A submission was where one of the wrestlers surrendered because a hold was too painful. But if the wrestler being held could manage to touch the ropes with a hand or a foot, the other wrestler had to release him.

The referee was dressed in a neat and gleaming all-white outfit of trousers and shirt, with a black tie. He brought the two trolls together in the centre of the ring and told them to shake hands.

For the first time, Jack noticed how big Mudd was. When he'd been at the registration desk with Big Rock, Jack had been too preoccupied over his row with Lord Veto to take much notice of Big Rock's opponent. Now, at last, he saw that Mudd was enormous, taller than Big Rock, and with long and muscular arms. And, as before, his body was covered in a slippery mud-like ooze.

'This isn't going to be easy for Big Rock,' Jack whispered to Milo.

'Nothing's easy,' whispered back Milo. 'But Big Rock's determined. He's got the most courageous heart you'll ever find.' Then he paused and added: 'Well, if trolls had hearts, that is.'

As the two trolls finished shaking hands, there was the sound of the bell and the crowd cheered and shouted even louder. It had begun!

Chapter 7

The two trolls moved into the centre of the ring, and immediately Mudd lashed out with a foot and tripped Big Rock. Big Rock tumbled, and Jack sucked in his breath as the huge Mudd dropped on Big Rock's head and shoulders, pinning him to the canvas.

'One!' shouted the referee. 'Two . . . !'

One of Big Rock's arms shot up into the air, showing he had a shoulder off the canvas. Mudd moved to push that shoulder down, and as he did so, Big Rock used the opportunity to slide out from beneath Mudd's body, roll away, and bounce to his feet.

'I thought Big Rock was caught then,' whispered Jack, worried.

'No,' grinned Milo. 'Big Rock's better than that.'

As Mudd got back to his feet, Big Rock suddenly dropped to the canvas and rolled towards Mudd like a big rolling stone, taking the huge troll's legs from under him. Mudd thudded to the canvas, and before he could get up, Big Rock had thrown himself onto his opponent, pinning him down.

'One . . . two . . . three!' roared the referee.

The crowd went wild, cheering and stamping their feet as the two trolls got up. The referee ordered them back to their own corners, and then signalled for them to start wrestling again.

This time Big Rock tried a charge, lowering his head and hurtling across the ring straight at Mudd, but Mudd dodged to one side. Jack was impressed at how fast the big troll moved for someone of his size. Jack was even more impressed when Mudd swung one of his huge arms into Big Rock's back as Big Rock stumbled past him and went flying through the ropes and out of the ring.

Big Rock crashed to the floor in front of the first row of the crowd.

'He's out of the ring!' said Jack, alarmed. 'If he doesn't get back before the count of ten ends, it'll be a knockout!'

Sure enough, the referee had already started the count. 'One. Two. Three. Four. Five . . .'

Big Rock pushed himself to his feet and stood, swaying slightly.

'Six. Seven. Eight . . .' counted the referee.

'He's dazed!' said Jack. 'He's not going to make it!'

Suddenly Big Rock lurched towards the ring, grabbed the top rope and pulled himself over it and back into the ring, just as the referee said: 'Nine!'

'He barely made it!' whispered Jack.

In the ring, Big Rock had recovered and threw himself at Mudd. He climbed up the other troll and wrapped both his legs around Mudd's neck. The crowd cheered and yelled, shouting for a submission from Mudd as Big Rock tightened the grip of his legs. But suddenly Mudd rolled forwards, taking Big Rock with him, and before Big Rock could disentangle himself, Big Rock was folded up on the canvas, with all Mudd's weight on him, as the referee counted, 'One! Two! Three!'

One pinfall each! The contest was level!

The two trolls got back to their feet, returned to their corners briefly, and then began to circle each other.

For the next fifteen minutes it was a stalemate in the ring. First Mudd held Big Rock down, but Big Rock managed to wriggle free and in turn held Mudd down.

Finally it looked as if it was all over for Big Rock when Mudd picked Big Rock up, turned him upside down, and slammed him down head first into the canvas with such force that the whole large tent vibrated. But, instead of collapsing into a heap, Big Rock stayed upright, upside down, and his hands shot out and grabbed hold of both of Mudd's ankles.

Before Mudd, or the crowd, realised what was happening, Big Rock had dropped down

and then stood up fast, swinging both hands
as he went, so Mudd swung round and round
in a circle, going faster and faster until both
trolls were almost a blur. And then Big Rock
let go.

Mudd hurtled away from Big Rock, hit one
of the corner posts, and bounced back towards
Big Rock. On his way past, Big Rock grabbed
the troll, turned him upside down, dropped him

on his back onto the canvas, and fell on him.

'One! Two!'

Jack wondered if Mudd was going to be able to lift a shoulder off the canvas, but all that whirling around had obviously made the big troll giddy, because he lay there as the referee called out, 'Three! And the winner, by two pinfalls, is Big Rock!'

Jack and Milo leapt to their feet, cheering and clapping, like the rest of the crowd in the tent. All except two.

As Jack jumped about happily, he noticed Lord Veto and Warg were deep in conversation; from the grim looks on their faces they were angry about something. And when Lord Veto got angry, as Jack knew from his years working at Veto Castle, trouble always followed.

As Big Rock did a victory parade around the ring, waving to the crowd, Jack moved away from Milo so he was near enough to Lord Veto and Warg to hear what they were saying. And what he heard confirmed his fears.

'This isn't looking good, Warg,' he heard Lord

Veto mutter. 'This Big Rock is better than I thought he'd be. On this form, he could actually beat Aggro!'

'It's only an exhibition bout, Lord Veto,' replied Warg. 'It's not a championship.'

'It doesn't matter, you fool!' Lord Veto snapped. 'If that troll beats Aggro tonight, then he'll have the right to challenge Aggro for the title! And if he wins that, my reputation as having the best wrestlers in the whole land will

be gone! My fortune is based on having the champion wrestlers in my stable!'

Jack saw Warg's eyes flickering as he thought this over.

'We have to stop the troll from winning,' Warg said.

'Of course we have to stop the troll from winning, you idiot!' growled Lord Veto. 'But how?'

A nasty smile appeared on the orc's face.

'Milo,' he said. And he began to whisper.

Chapter 8

Milo put the prize money he'd just received for Big Rock winning the contest into his inside pocket, and smiled happily. With that, plus the cash he'd be picking up later from the Wrestling Federation as their share of the ticket money, the gang would be set up for a while. They'd be able to buy some good food – or maybe some good ingredients for Jack to turn into a fantastic meal – and some sweet hay for Robin, and maybe even a new costume for Big Rock; his old one was starting to look a bit worn and there were holes appearing where holes shouldn't be.

As Milo headed for the exit to join the rest of the crew at the caravan, he found his way barred by the large figure of Warg, Lord Veto's Chief Orc. Along with Warg there were three other orcs, all wrestlers. Milo recognised their style: long arms ready to attack, claws at the ready.

'Lord Veto would like to have a private word with you,' said Warg.

Four orcs, thought Milo. It doesn't take four Wrestling Orcs to bring me a message. There's something bad going on here, and I get the feeling I might be the target.

'No problem,' said Milo. 'I'll be in our caravan. He can find me there.'

Milo started to move off, but two of the orcs held out their long arms to stop him. Warg and the other orc were also standing very close to him.

'Lord Veto would prefer to see you at the castle,' said Warg.

'Still no problem,' nodded Milo. 'Let's go to my caravan. I'll check my diary and we can fix an appointment.'

Again, Milo started to walk off, but once more the two large orcs moved swiftly sideways, cutting off his line of escape.

'Lord Veto would like to talk to you now,' said Warg firmly.

'Sorry,' said Milo, shaking his head. 'I'm busy right now. Big Rock's got a bout to prepare for.'

And this time, as the twin orcs once more slid sideways to try to block his exit, Milo moved nimbly backwards. But he wasn't nimble enough. The third orc was already there,

blocking him.

'Big –!' Milo began to yell, but before he could say the word 'Rock', the orc's huge claw-like hand closed over his mouth, cutting off any further sound, and Milo found himself being lifted off the ground and his arms trapped as his coat was pulled down to his elbows.

Chapter 9

Lord Veto watched his favourite Wrestling Orc, Aggro, National Wrestling Champion, train. This part of his training took the form of members of Lord Veto's castle staff hurling themselves at Aggro, and Aggro grabbing them and throwing them out of the ring. So far two butlers, three gardeners and five stable-hands lay on the ground outside the ring, groaning and clutching different parts of themselves in agony. Some of them wouldn't be able to work as well as they normally did for a few days, so it could be expensive in staff numbers. But then, Lord Veto didn't pay big wages, and he could always get more people from the estate to do the jobs.

As he watched Aggro hurl another gardener out of the ring, Lord Veto reflected that this sort of training was all well and good for developing Aggro's fast reflexes, but it wouldn't be much use when the orc was up against Big Rock. The Wrestling Troll was good. Possibly too good. Even though it was only an exhibition bout, as he'd told Warg, he couldn't afford for Aggro to lose.

'My Lord,' murmured a voice just behind him.

Lord Veto turned. Warg was there.

'Well?' he asked.

Warg smiled.

'It's done,' he said.

'Excellent!' said Lord Veto.

Big Rock sat on the steps of the caravan, his rocky face even more creased than usual as he gave a puzzled frown.

'Milo never been this long before when he collect prize money,' he said.

Jack paced around in a small circle in agitation. Robin looked up from grazing and said, 'Will you stop that! You going round and round like that is making me feel dizzy!'

'Something bad has happened to Milo!' said Jack. 'I should have made him take us with him to get the prize money. Lord Veto is behind this!'

'Did I hear my name?' murmured a voice.

Jack stopped pacing and whirled round. Lord

Veto and his orc, Warg, had appeared as if out of nowhere.

Jack and Robin looked at the pair warily.

'You seem concerned,' said Lord Veto.

Jack recognised that sneaky silkiness in Lord Veto's voice, which meant that Veto was feeling very smug about something, and that something had to be very nasty.

'We can't find Milo,' said Big Rock.

'Really?' said Lord Veto. 'Well, that's a coincidence. It's your friend Milo that I've come to see you about.'

'Do you know where he is?' demanded Jack.

Lord Veto turned to Jack and sneered nastily: 'I wasn't talking to you, kitchen boy.'

'Do you know where he is?' demanded Big Rock.

'Yes, I do, actually,' said Lord Veto. 'He's being looked after by a few of my Wrestling Orcs.'

'Looked after?' echoed Jack, shocked.

Lord Veto ignored Jack and addressed himself to Big Rock.

'His safety is my concern,' he added.

'Oh, that all right then,' nodded Big Rock. He turned to Jack and said: 'Milo being looked after. He okay.'

'At the moment,' added Lord Veto menacingly.

'Good,' nodded Big Rock. Again, he said to Jack: 'Milo okay. Everything good.'

Lord Veto let out a groan of exasperation and said to Warg, 'These trolls are really thick aren't they.'

'What?' asked Big Rock, puzzled.

'He's threatening us,' said Jack, his face white with anger. 'He's threatening Milo.'

'Thank you,' nodded Lord Veto. 'At least one of you is getting the message. Perhaps you'd explain it to the large lump of rock next to you.'

Big Rock frowned, baffled. 'Don't get it,' he said. 'He say Milo okay. Being looked after.'

'But he's saying it in a way that suggests he's got Milo somewhere and he's planning to hurt him unless we do what he wants.'

'Exactly!' said Lord Veto. 'Big Rock needs

to lose against Aggro, of course. I would have thought that was obvious. Otherwise, I might be forced to use your friend as a training aid for my Wrestling Orcs.' He gave a nasty smile. 'If that happens, they'll tear him apart.'

Big Rock gave a snarl of anger, the first time Jack had ever heard him make such a sound, and he reached out to grab hold of Lord Veto, who darted backwards and hid behind Warg.

'Lay a finger on me and your friend Milo will suffer for it!' snapped Lord Veto.

Big Rock growled again and advanced towards Warg and Lord Veto, but Jack stepped in his way.

'No, Big Rock,' cautioned Jack. 'He means it.'

'It's good that one of you has some sense,' said Lord Veto. 'So, that's my offer. Lose against Aggro, and your friend goes free. Win, and you'll never see him alive again.'

With that, Lord Veto and the orc turned and walked away.

Big Rock let out another low rumbling growl

of anger, and then – to Jack's surprise – the growl turned into a sound like bubbles bursting.

Jack looked at the huge troll, and realised that there were wet marks on Big Rock's cheeks. The Wrestling Troll was crying.

'Milo my friend!' said Big Rock brokenly. He let out a heavy sigh that was so big the ground beneath their feet shook. 'I got to lose.'

'Lose!' said an indignant voice behind them.

Big Rock and Jack turned, and saw Robin the horse standing looking at them accusingly.

'Is that what Milo would want you to do?' demanded the horse. 'To lose a wrestling match on purpose? Is that in the spirit of Wrestling Trolls?'

'No,' admitted Big Rock. 'But they got Milo!'

'Then get him back!' said Robin. He grunted. 'Lose a wrestling match on purpose, indeed! I've never heard anything so terrible in all my years!'

'But how?' asked Big Rock helplessly. 'We don't know where they got Milo!'

'Yes we do!' said Jack. 'There's only one place

they'd put him, and that's in the dungeons at Veto Castle.'

'Dungeons!' groaned Big Rock. 'We never get him out!'

'Yes we will!' said Jack determinedly. 'Don't forget, I spent my whole life in the castle. I know all the cellars and corridors and tunnels, and every part of that place. I'll go down to the dungeons and rescue Milo.'

'On your own?' asked Robin sarcastically.

'Yes,' said Jack. 'Because the best time to do it will be tonight when Big Rock's in the ring with Aggro. Most of Lord Veto's people will be watching the match, so there'll only be a couple of guards left to watch over the dungeons.'

'Yes, that's good thinking,' Robin admitted. Then he gave a snort of doubt. 'But I can't see you on your own beating even just a couple of guards. They'll have weapons and armour.' The old horse shook his shaggy head. 'You're going to need help. I'll come with you.'

Chapter 10

Jack and Robin stood at the back of the huge tent, watching the crowd, listening to their roars and cheers as Big Rock pulled himself into the ring.

Aggro the Orc was already in the ring, standing in the centre, waving at the crowd, while the supporters of both wrestlers tried to outshout the other.

'Aggro! Aggro, Aggro!' and, 'Orcs! Orcs! Orcs!' yelled one part of the crowd, while the opposing section roared and chanted, 'Big Rock! Big Rock, Big Rock!' and, 'Trolls! Trolls! Trolls!'

The whole place was a sea of waving placards and pumping fists. Most of the placards had a picture of a mountaintop on them, for Big Rock, and others had a claw that was the traditional sign of the Wrestling Orcs, but some of the placards, mainly the homemade ones drawn on bits of cardboard, had messages such as MORE GOBLINS! and one said MY NAME IS HENRY!

'I wish I could stay and support him,' said Jack sadly, as he looked at Big Rock standing in his corner.

'So does he,' said Robin. 'But we've got a job to do.'

Two fans had burst out from the crowded seats and were waving a huge banner that read AGGRO: NATIONAL CHAMPION – THE BEST OF THE BEST!

At this, half of the crowd went wild, yelling and stamping their feet, while Big Rock's supporters started booing and shouting for the fans with the banner to sit down.

'Now,' said Robin. 'While everyone's watching the action.'

Robin moved silently off through the tent

flap. Jack cast one last look at Big Rock, a lonely figure standing on his own in the ring, and then followed the horse.

Big Rock felt unhappy. In all his time as a wrestler, he'd always had someone in his corner, urging him on, encouraging him. First there had been Waldo, then there had been Milo. Tonight, there was no one. Big Rock was on his own and it felt very strange and very uncomfortable for him.

Aggro strode from his position at the centre of the ring right up to Big Rock and sneered, wagging one of his claws in the troll's face. 'You are gone, troll!' he snarled. 'I'm gonna finish you off in the first round!'

No, thought Big Rock. The first round won't give Jack and Robin time to find Milo and free him. I have to keep this match going for two rounds at least. Maybe three. Maybe four. Maybe . . .

Big Rock's brain struggled with what came after four. He wasn't very good with numbers. He thought it might be five. Or was it six?

Whatever it was, he had to keep the Orc Champion going until Jack and Robin returned with Milo.

As Aggro walked to his corner, where Warg was waiting for him, Big Rock looked down at the audience. Lord Veto was sitting in the middle of the front row, looking very important. Lord Veto glanced up at Big Rock, smiled a nasty smile and winked.

No, this match isn't going to go how you think, thought Big Rock determinedly. Providing Jack and Robin could rescue Milo.

The bell sounded for round one, and the audience went wild, cheering and shouting and stamping as Big Rock and Aggro moved to the centre of the ring.

Jack and Robin went carefully down the stone steps of the castle that led to the dungeons. When they reached the bottom, Jack stopped and listened. In front of them were three tunnels, dimly lit by flaming torches set in the walls. They heard a muttering from one of the tunnels.

'That'll be the guards talking,' whispered Jack. 'And where there are guards, there'll be a prisoner.'

Jack set off down the tunnel, Robin following. Two guards were outside one of the dungeon doors.

'Just our luck to be stuck here when there's wrestling,' complained one unhappily.

'Arr!' agreed the other guard.

Then both guards became aware of Jack and Robin bearing down on them.

'What do you want?' demanded one of the guards. Then he peered closer at Jack through the gloom. 'I know you! You're that kitchen boy, ain't you?'

'Yes,' said Jack. 'Lord Veto sent us. He wants to see the prisoner. We're to take him to Lord Veto.'

The guards looked at one another, exchanging puzzled frowns.

'He never said anything about that to us, did he, Bill?' said one.

'No,' said Bill. 'In fact he told us to make

sure the prisoner didn't leave the dungeon under any circumstances. Ain't that right, Ben?'

'That is,' nodded Ben.

'Well, he changed his mind,' said Jack.

Bill and Ben looked unconvinced.

'That don't sound like Lord Veto to me,' said Bill.

'No it don't,' said Ben. 'And we'll need an order from Lord Veto before we can release

the prisoner.'

'In writing,' added Bill. 'Lord Veto was very particular about that. "Don't let the prisoner leave without a written order from me," he told us.'

'Okay,' said Jack. 'I'll go and get a written order.'

'And it's got to have his seal on it,' said Ben. 'You know, that big wax blob, with the impression of his ring pressed into it. As proof that the order's from him.'

Drat! thought Jack.

'Look, we don't have time to get the order and get him to put his seal on it,' said Jack. 'Lord Veto's very busy right now watching the wrestling. So if you'll just give us the prisoner . . .'

Bill and Ben stared at Jack. 'Give you the prisoner?' they echoed.

'Yes,' said Jack.

'Without an official written order?' said Bill.

'No,' said Ben. 'Absolutely not. That's more than our jobs are worth.' Then he looked at

Robin with a puzzled frown. 'And why have you brought a horse down here with you?'

'To kick that door down if you clowns don't open it,' snapped Robin impatiently. To Jack he said: 'We don't have time for this. Big Rock will be being clobbered up in that ring. We need to do this quickly.'

'Do what?' asked Ben.

Jack pointed at the dungeon door. 'Open that door now!' he ordered. 'Or else you'll be sorry.'

Bill and Ben both shook their heads. 'Oh no we won't,' they said. And Bill produced a short spear, and Ben a sword. 'You're the ones who are going to be sorry!'

Jack and Robin glared at the two armed guards, standing resolute in front of the dungeon door. From inside the dungeon they heard Milo's voice call out: 'What's going on out there? Is that you, Jack?'

'Yes!' Jack called back. 'Me and Robin are here to get you out!'

'It shouldn't take long!' added Robin. 'There are only these two guards.' And then he reared up and flailed his front feet at the guards, who quailed back. 'And I've got my hooves!'

'But are they a match for six Wrestling Orcs?' growled a savage voice behind them.

Chapter 11

In the ring, the crowd yelled and cheered as Big Rock slammed Aggro into the canvas. The big orc snarled as he got to his feet and glared at Big Rock, and then leapt at the troll, raking his claws across Big Rock's chest, making sparks. Under the cover of the shower of sparks, so the referee couldn't see, the orc poked the point of one of his claws hard into one of Big Rock's eyes.

Big Rock stumbled back, feeling pain and being momentarily blinded.

Aggro was cheating. Big Rock had expected that; orcs always cheated. But the claw in his eye had caught him by surprise.

Aggro took advantage of Big Rock being

blinded and launched an attack, kicking and punching. Under the weight of the blows and kicks, Big Rock lost his balance and fell to the canvas, but just managed to roll clear in time as Aggro dropped onto the space where the troll had been lying.

Big Rock ended up by the edge of the ring, and as his vision cleared he found himself looking at the angry face of Lord Veto.

'You're not losing, troll!' snarled Lord Veto in a harsh whisper. 'You've got one minute to lose this fight, or I send Warg to kill your friend.'

'You kill Milo, I kill you!' warned Big Rock.

Suddenly Big Rock felt his ankles grabbed and he was pulled back into the centre of the ring by the orc. Aggro released his grip on Big Rock's ankles, and suddenly jumped hard on Big Rock's back. Big Rock felt one of his rock ribs break.

Ow! he thought. Then he said to himself: must keep going for Milo's sake.

* * *

Jack and Robin turned, and saw with a shock that there were indeed six huge Wrestling Orcs who'd crept up silently behind them.

'Lord Veto noticed that you weren't in your troll's corner,' said the leading orc. 'So he sent us down in case you were thinking of trying something silly.'

'Like freeing your friend from the dungeons,' said another of the orcs.

'So, are you going to arrest them?' asked Bill.

'Arrest them?' chuckled one of the orcs. 'Orcs don't arrest people.'

'We eat them!' said another nastily.

With that, the orcs snarled, showing their sharp teeth, and flexed their claws as they moved towards Jack and Robin.

This is it, thought Jack, his heart sinking. After all these years, finally I stand up to Lord Veto and his orcs, and I'm going to be killed! And eaten! He'd seen orcs in a fighting frenzy. There'd be nothing left of him after this but bones!

Jack backed away, and as he did so he began to experience the same odd sensation he'd felt just before Warg had thrown him into the puddle: a kind of mist began to fill his mind, crystals began to appear before his eyes, and he felt a shuddering sensation pumping through his arms and legs.

Robin rose up on his hind legs again, waving his forefeet at the orcs.

'You think you can eat me?' he demanded.

'I'm too tough for you! And I'll take at least three of you with me! These horseshoes are made of solid iron!'

To his delight, and surprise, the orcs stopped, and he saw worried looks appear on their faces.

Got you! he thought. Scared of an old horse, eh!

And then he noticed that they weren't looking at him, but over his head at something high up behind him.

Puzzled, Robin turned, and let out a gasp. There, where Jack had been standing was . . . well, a troll. But more than an ordinary troll. This one was huge, bigger even than Big Rock, and looked to be made of solid stone all the way up to . . .

Robin gaped.

The head of the troll wasn't a normal troll's head. It was large and made of some sort of stone, but there was something . . . human-looking about it. And, as Robin watched, the troll's mouth opened and a roar came out, a huge terrifying roar. The orcs took a step back, their mouths open in awe. And then the huge troll moved forwards, faster than Robin had ever seen a troll move. The troll's fists flashed once, twice, three times … and three of the orcs were suddenly lying unconscious on the floor.

Bang! Another lash of a fist, and a fourth orc crumpled to the ground.

That was too much for the remaining two orcs. They turned and ran. As did Bill and Ben, the two guards.

'What's happening?' demanded Milo from behind the dungeon door.

'I'll tell you in a minute,' said Robin. 'Where's the key to the door?'

'The guards have got it,' said Milo.

Great, groaned Robin to himself.

'Okay,' he said. 'Stand back. I'm going to try to kick it down.'

Robin turned so that his back was to the door.

One good strong kick, he told himself. It had been years since he'd done that sort of thing, but he was sure he still could. Even though the dungeon door looked pretty strong and thick. Still, they had to get Milo out, and this was obviously the only way.

CRASH!

Robin frowned. He hadn't even moved, yet he heard a splintering sound behind him. He looked over his shoulder.

The door to the dungeon lay in splinters.

Milo came cautiously out from the dungeon, stepping over the broken bits of wood.

'Wow!' he said. 'That was some powerful

kick!'

'That wasn't me,' said Robin. 'It was him.'

Milo turned, and saw the towering figure of the troll.

'Who's that?' asked Milo.

'Jack,' said Robin.

'Jack?' asked Milo. 'Jack who?'

'Our Jack. The boy who cooks.'

Milo stared at the huge powerful figure, stunned. The huge figure began to shrink and change . . . and suddenly Jack was standing there. He looked dazed.

'What . . . what happened?' he asked. He looked at the shattered dungeon door, and then at Milo and Robin. 'Who did that?' he asked.

'It's a long story,' said Milo.

'Which we'll tell you later,' said Robin. 'Right now, jump on my back! We have to get back to the wrestling ring and save Big Rock!'

Chapter 12

Smash! Crash!

Aggro's head thudded into Big Rock's face.

The troll had been tangled up in the ropes by the orc, and although the referee had tried to intervene, Aggro had taken the opportunity to headbutt Big Rock twice before the referee ordered the orc away.

Aggro walked around the ring, smirking and smiling, waving to his fans. There had still been no pinfalls or submissions, but the orc's cheating tactics were starting to have an effect on Big Rock, wearing him down. As Big Rock struggled to free himself from the ropes, Aggro pointed to something outside the ring and the referee turned to look. While the referee's back was turned, Aggro swung round and landed a vicious kick high on Big Rock's chest, sending the troll right through the ropes and out of the ring.

Big Rock's supporters immediately sent up a chorus of boos and yells of, 'Cheat! Cheat!' while Aggro's supporters yelled: 'Out of the ring! Knockout!'

The referee turned and saw Big Rock lying on the floor and began the count: 'One. Two. Three. Four. Five . . .'

'Big Rock!'

The troll pushed himself up, dazed, doing his best to focus, and saw that the person speaking to him was . . . Milo!

'Milo?' he said.

'Yes!' said Milo urgently. Behind Milo were Jack and Robin. 'Now get back in the ring and finish this!'

'Six!' shouted the referee. 'Seven! Eight!'

Big Rock pushed himself to his feet, let out a roar that filled the whole of the tent, and leapt from outside the ring over the ropes, landing right in the centre.

Aggro frowned, a look of doubt on the orc's face. This shouldn't be happening.

Before Aggro could stop him, Big Rock had reached down, grabbed hold of the orc by the knees and then straightened, throwing Aggro as far and as hard as he could.

This time it was the orc who sailed through the air, and he crashed down on the rows of audience, who just managed to scramble clear in time. The orc lay among the wreckage of the rows of seats and heard the referee begin the count: 'One. Two. Three.'

Aggro let out a snarl of anger and began to lurch upright, and then found that he couldn't. One of his big claws had got caught under a long row of the wrecked seats, the metal bars trapping it.

'Four. Five. Six.'

'No!' yelled Aggro, and he began to tug at the metal holding him back.

'Seven. Eight.'

With a last burst of energy, Aggro lifted the metal bars and began to run back towards the ring, trampling over the audience in his mad rush to get back into it.

'Nine . . .'

The orc was stretching to reach for the ropes as the referee's voice called out: 'Ten!'

The audience erupted.

'Yessss!' yelled Milo and Jack, and then hugged one another and began to jump up and down.

In the ring, the referee was holding up Big Rock's arm and saying, 'The winner: Big Rock!' but no one could hear him over the massive amount of noise in the tent.

As Milo, Big Rock, Jack and Robin headed towards the exit, they passed Lord Veto and Warg. Lord Veto glared at them with such anger that, if looks could kill, they would all have been dead on the spot.

'This isn't over!' snarled Lord Veto.

'I think it is,' grinned Milo. 'Unless you fancy a rematch – your champion against Big Rock?'

Lord Veto scowled. As Milo, Big Rock, Jack

and Robin moved away, he called after them: 'And who's that new Wrestling Troll? The one who wrecked the door of my dungeon!'

'Him?' shrugged Milo. He winked. 'At the moment he's a secret. But you'll see him soon enough. Maybe in the ring.' He gave another big smile. 'Anyway, can't stay and chat, Lord Veto, we've got to go and collect our winnings for Big Rock beating your Aggro.'

With that, Milo, Big Rock, Jack and Robin walked off.

Lord Veto gave a low snarl. 'It isn't over, you peasant!' he growled. 'Trust me, I'll have my own back on you and your Wrestling Trolls!'

WRESTLING TROLLS
TO THE RESCUE

Chapter 1

The caravan with wwт on it creaked as it moved slowly along the country road. In front, pulling the caravan, plodded the old shaggy horse, Robin. Big Rock, the Wrestling Troll, ran behind the caravan, overtook it, ran round it, ran backwards, and then ran round the caravan again, all the time throwing punches at the empty air. He was training.

In the driving seat of the caravan sat Milo and Jack. Milo held the horse's reins and sang:

'Wrestling Trolls.
Tum-di-dum!
Wrestling Trolls.
Tum-di-dum!'

Milo turned to the glum-looking Jack and said, 'Come on! Join in the song! It'll make you feel good!'

'Nothing will make me feel good!' groaned Jack. 'I turned into a Wrestling Troll!' Hastily he added, so as not to upset Big Rock, 'Not that there's anything wrong with trolls, I love Wrestling Trolls. I just don't understand why

it happened. It's weird, and I'm worried it'll happen again.'

'So what?' said Milo. 'It was lucky for us it happened. You saved us!'

'Yes, but I don't know if it'll happen again!' He let out another sigh. 'Anyway, I don't know the words to the song.'

'There aren't any words,' said Milo. 'Well, there are, but that's all of them:

> 'Wrestling Trolls.
> 'Tum-di-dum!
> 'Wrestling Trolls.
> 'Tum-di-dum!

'And you just keep singing it over and over.'

'Until the poor creature pulling the caravan can't stand it any more,' grumbled Robin.

'It's a good song!' defended Milo. 'My uncle Waldo wrote it!'

'How can you claim he wrote it,' demanded Robin, 'when the only words in it are: Wrestling Trolls. Tum-di-dum!? That's not writing a song, that's . . .' The old horse struggled to find the right words and finally came up with: 'Stupid.'

'It's not stupid!' said Milo. 'It's a good song because everyone can sing it!'

'Trolls sang it when we had lots of trolls,' agreed Big Rock as he ran past. 'It good song!'

Then he disappeared again, running backwards.

Milo gave Jack a cheerful smile. 'So, what do you think we should call you?' he asked.

Jack looked at him with a puzzled frown. 'Jack,' he said. 'That's my name.'

'I mean when you're . . . you know . . . the other you. The big one. The . . . er . . .'

'Troll,' said Jack, and sighed again.

'Yes,' nodded Milo. 'When you're . . . him.'

'How about Thud?' suggested the horse.

'Thud?' asked Milo.

'It was the sound that door made as it came off its hinges,' said Robin. 'And so did Lord Veto's orcs when they hit the floor.'

'I like it,' said Milo. 'It has a good ring to it. Perfect for a Wrestling Troll.'

'But I'm not a Wrestling Troll,' said Jack. 'I'm

Jack. I'm a boy.'

'And that's a perfect name for you when you're a boy,' nodded Milo. 'But when you're . . . him. That big, tough, troll-like guy. He looks and sounds to me like Thud.'

'He certainly did when we were in those dungeons,' added Robin. He chuckled. 'Thud. Biff. Bash. And Thud again.'

'Excellent,' smiled Milo. 'That's you. You're Thud.'

'I'm not!' insisted Jack. 'I bet it won't ever happen again.'

'It'd be great if it did,' said Milo. 'Big Rock and Thud. Two Wrestling Trolls!' He frowned. 'I wonder what caused it? Have you ever seen anything like that before, Big Rock?'

'No,' said Big Rock, and he danced past them, throwing punches and kicks at the air as he went.

'What about you, Robin? You're a horse who's seen a lot. Especially with Wrestling Trolls.'

Robin frowned. 'I'll think about it,' he said.

'Right now, I'm going to stop talking because we have a hill coming up, and I need my breath to haul this heavy caravan up it.'

'We could always get off and make it lighter,' said Milo.

'That is a very good idea,' said Robin.

'And while we're off, I could always fix us a quick snack to give you energy,' suggested Jack.

Robin stopped, and if a horse could have been said to smile, then Robin was smiling. 'That,' he said, 'is an even better idea!'

Chapter 2

Lunch for Milo, Robin and Jack was a pie, made by Jack. Big Rock munched on a selection of tiny stones of different shades and colours, now and then taking a bigger bite out of a chunk of granite.

After lunch, the gang packed up and set off, with Big Rock once again running backwards and forwards around the caravan.

'Where's this place we're going to?' asked Jack.

'It's a town called Weevil,' said Milo.

'Has it got good wrestling?' asked Jack.

'Of course it has!' said Milo. 'Remember that special VIP guest at the Trolls versus Orcs Slamdown last week?'

'Princess Ava,' nodded Jack, remembering the small girl who'd been in the royal box.

'That's her,' said Milo. 'Well, Weevil is her kingdom. She loves wrestling. Her father, the old king, loved wrestling as well.' He smiled. 'I came here years ago with my uncle Waldo and the Wrestling Trolls, and it was great!'

'Good wrestling,' agreed Big Rock as he ran past, punching the air with his enormous fists.

By now they had reached the outskirts of the small town, and the wheels of the caravan left the dust of the earth road and began to rattle over the cobbles of the streets. The place looked pretty deserted, just a few people hurrying by, and all of them keeping their eyes down towards the ground. They trundled on through the cobbled streets until they reached the market square in the town centre. As in the rest of the town, only a few people were in the square, and none of them were hanging about.

'Strange,' muttered Milo. 'When we were here before this place was really busy. Loads of people. I wonder where everyone is?'

Big Rock pointed to a large building at one side of the square. 'That where wrestling was last time,' he said.

'Yes,' said Milo.

Now they saw that the doors of the building had been nailed shut, and there was a large closed sign placed over them.

'Strange,' murmured Milo again.

He saw a woman walking along, accompanied by three small children aged from about eight

down to just three years old.

'Excuse me!' called Milo.

The woman stopped and looked at him and the caravan and especially Big Rock with suspicion.

'Yes?' she asked.

'We're looking for the wrestling tournament –'

He didn't get a chance to finish. The woman uttered a shocked gasp and put her hands over the ears of her youngest child. The middle child pointed an accusing finger at Milo and shouted, 'Bad men! Bad men!'

'Hush!' said his mother, and swept her children away as fast as she could.

Milo turned to Jack. 'What did I say?' he demanded, bewildered.

'You said the "w" word,' muttered a voice.

They turned and saw that a man had appeared by the caravan. He was tall and powerful-looking with a battered face, and that face had a very unhappy expression.

'What do you mean?' asked Jack. 'Wrest—'

'Sssh!' snapped the man, and he looked

around nervously. When he was satisfied that there was no one else around to overhear, he turned back to Milo, Jack, Big Rock and Robin. 'You must be strangers here.'

'Well, yes,' admitted Milo, 'but I came here years ago with my uncle Waldo.' He gestured at Big Rock. 'With Big Rock here, and my uncle's other Wrestling Trolls.'

'Don't say that word!' said the man warningly.

'Trolls?' queried Big Rock, puzzled.

'I think he means the other word, Big Rock,' murmured Jack. 'The "w" one.'

'Exactly,' nodded the man. 'Everything about it is banned here. The sport itself. And worse, anyone who looks like a . . .' and here he dropped his voice to a whisper: 'wrestler, or is thought of as having anything to do with wrestling, gets arrested and locked up.'

'Why?' asked Milo, still looking bewildered. 'When we were last here everyone loved w— . . . it.'

'Yes, they did,' said the man. 'I used to be a . . . sportsman myself.' He pointed at his battered face. 'Which is where I got this face.'

'It good face,' said Big Rock.

'Not any more,' sighed the man. 'Because I look like a . . . sportsman . . . the townsfolk treat me with suspicion.' He looked gloomy. 'I've thought of moving to somewhere else, where . . . sport . . . is still allowed.' He sighed unhappily again. 'But I was born here. I like this town. It was a great and happy town until

General Pepper took over last week.' He shook his head sadly. 'Just one week, and this whole place has become a nightmare to live in!'

'A week?!' echoed Milo, shocked.

'Who's General Pepper?' asked Jack.

'He's Princess Ava's uncle,' said the man.

'But she was guest of honour at the last wrest— er, sporting tournament,' said Milo. 'I thought she loved wrest— er . . . sports?'

'She does,' nodded the man. 'She's absolutely mad on it. That was one of the reasons for the row between her and her uncle. He hates it, but she wanted to set up a school for . . . wrestlers. But General Pepper didn't want her spending any money on it, so when she came back from that . . . sporting tournament . . . he had her locked up at the top of a tall tower, and then took over as ruler of the region.'

'How did he get away with that?' asked Jack. 'Didn't anyone object? Wasn't Princess Ava popular?'

'Princess Ava was very popular,' said the man. 'When she was locked up some people talked about breaking Princess Ava out of her prison and overthrowing General Pepper. Especially those people who liked . . . sports. But that was before the General's soldiers went into action. And there are lots of them, heavily armed, enforcing the General's new laws banning . . . sports . . . and everything and everyone to do with it.'

'That's terrible!' said Jack.

Suddenly they heard a shout, and turned to see a troop of ten soldiers, all armed with spears, approaching. At their front was their leader, carrying a sword and wearing a captain's armour.

'You lot!' called the Captain. 'We've had complaints about you! We have reason to believe that you are involved in the criminal act of wrestling!'

Chapter 3

Milo looked at the Captain and the armed soldiers and laughed out loud.

'Us?' he chuckled. 'Good heavens, no! Nothing to do with us!'

'Then why did you ask where the wrestling tournament was?' demanded the Captain.

Jack and Milo noticed that the woman and her children they'd talked to earlier were now standing just behind the soldiers, watching them. Jack also noticed that the big man they'd been talking to had slipped quietly away.

'Well?' demanded the Captain accusingly. 'Did you ask where the wrestling was?'

'Er . . .' began Milo.

'Yes he did!' called out the little boy. 'Bad

men! Bad men!'

'No, we're not bad men,' said Milo. 'We're after bad men. We're bounty hunters. We catch wrestlers and bring them to justice. We heard that wrestling was against the law here, so we thought we'd find out where the wrestlers were, arrest them, and bring them to General Pepper and get a bounty.'

The Captain looked at Milo suspiciously. Then at Jack, and Robin, and finally at Big Rock. 'That troll looks like a wrestler to me,' he snapped. 'A Wrestling Troll.'

'No, no!' said Milo quickly. 'He's . . . He's a bounty hunter. We knew the people we'd be up against would be big and tough, so we had to find someone just as big and tough. That's Big Rock, the bounty hunter.'

The Captain regarded Milo and Big Rock suspiciously. Then he said, 'We don't want bounty hunters in this town. We keep the law here. Me and my men. You'd better leave.'

'We will,' nodded Milo. 'We'll be on our way immediately.'

'We can't,' put in Jack. He pointed at Robin. 'Our horse is very old. He needs to rest before we can move on.'

As if to emphasise this point, Robin let out a long and weary groan and sank to his knees.

'See?' said Jack.

The Captain looked at Robin, then nodded. 'All right,' he said reluctantly. 'But you leave town first thing in the morning.'

With that, the Captain turned, barked an

order at the soldiers, and they marched away.

'What are you doing?' demanded Milo to Jack, annoyed. 'We need to get out of here now!'

'We can't,' said Jack, his tone serious.

'Yes we can!' retorted Milo.

Suddenly they noticed that the large man with the battered face had reappeared.

'See?' said the large man. 'That was Captain Oz, General Pepper's right-hand man. As long as they're in charge, this is going to be a terrible town.'

'Who are you?' asked Milo. 'And where did you disappear to?'

'My name's Sam Dent,' said the man.

'Sam Dent!' said Big Rock, and he looked at the man with new awe and respect. 'Famous Sam Dent! Great wrestler!'

'Not any more,' said Sam Dent ruefully.

'You know what we have to do,' said Jack determinedly.

'Yes,' said Milo. 'Leave town.'

'No,' said Jack. 'We have to rescue Princess

Ava. That's why Robin and I pulled that stunt about him being tired so we could stay.'

'No,' said Robin. 'I really am tired.'

'It won't be easy,' said Sam. 'There are armed soldiers guarding the entrance to the tower to make sure that no one can get in.'

'That shouldn't stop us!' insisted Jack. 'Once Princess Ava is out of prison, I bet you the people will unite behind her. And then she can banish General Pepper and his soldiers into exile. And then there'll be wrestling here again, as there ought to be.'

'No!' said Milo firmly. 'It's too dangerous. We'll be putting ourselves at risk against a load of armed soldiers, all for a Princess we've never seen.'

'We did see her,' said Jack. 'She was in the royal box at that tournament at Lord Veto's. She was the guest of honour.'

'I don't care,' said Milo. 'We don't know her personally. I say we leave as soon as we've rested up for the night.'

'No,' said Big Rock.

Milo and Jack looked at the big troll.

'What?' asked Milo.

'Jack right. Girl in trouble,' said Big Rock. 'Bad man in charge here. Ban wrestling. We rescue girl, like Jack say. Bring wrestling back.'

Milo let out a long sigh. 'Look, Big Rock, it's not that I'm unsympathetic to this Princess, and obviously I will always fight for the freedom to wrestle, but –'

'You're scared,' said Robin.

'No,' said Milo. 'I'm just being careful about our safety. Big Rock, Jack, Robin, you're all my responsibility . . .'

'We rescue girl,' said Big Rock firmly.

'. . . and, as I'm in charge of this outfit . . .' continued Milo.

'Me and Big Rock will rescue the Princess,' said Jack.

'I'll help,' offered Sam Dent.

'And me,' said Robin.

Milo stopped and looked at them all. Then he gave a shrug.

'Yes,' he said. 'That's what I was about to say.'

Chapter 4

'We won't be able to rescue the Princess easily with just us against all these soldiers,' pointed out Jack. 'We need a plan.'

They all fell silent and looked at one another questioningly.

'Don't look at me,' shrugged Robin. 'I'm just a horse.'

'Maybe we can use the General's new law as part of our plan,' Milo said.

'How?' asked Sam.

'What we need are two wrestlers,' said Milo. 'They start a wrestling match in the town square. That'll bring all the townspeople in to see it, and all the guards will come in to stop it. And, while that's going on and everyone's attention is on the match, Jack and me get into the tower and rescue the Princess!'

'That brilliant!' said Big Rock. Then he frowned. 'But who do wrestling match?'

'Well, as Jack and I will be in the tower rescuing the Princess, and as Robin can't wrestle –'

'Me!' beamed Big Rock. 'Wrestling Troll!'

'But you can't have a match with just one wrestler,' Jack pointed out. 'He needs an opponent.'

'Yes,' nodded Milo. And he looked at Sam.

Sam was silent for a moment, then he sighed heavily and said, 'I could go to jail.'

'Then we rescue you,' said Big Rock.

'That's what I like about Big Rock,' said Milo. 'He always sees everything so simply.'

Milo and Jack followed the directions from Sam, walking through main streets and side streets, until they came to the foot of a tall stone tower.

'There it is,' said Milo.

Jack nodded towards the six armed soldiers, each carrying a long spear and a sword, who took turns patrolling in front of the entrance to the tower, always leaving one soldier standing guard right in front of the door.

'Six against two,' said Jack. 'That's not good odds.'

'Do you think you could turn into Thud?' asked Milo hopefully. 'That would do the trick.'

'I don't know,' said Jack. 'When it happened before, I got this tickly sensation, and my eyes went sort of misty, like I was looking through very thick glass.'

'Any tickly feelings at the moment?' asked Milo.

'No,' said Jack.

Milo sighed.

'Maybe it'll happen once we go into action,' he said.

'Hopefully it won't come to that,' said Jack. 'Once they hear there's wrestling going on in the town centre, they're bound to rush off.'

'Say they don't?' asked Milo, concerned.

In the town square, Big Rock and Sam stood, sizing one another up.

'Proper wrestling rules,' said Big Rock. 'No cheating.'

'I never cheat,' said Sam indignantly.

Robin looked around the town square. It was empty. The horse guessed that most people had seen these two large characters standing opposite one another, flexing their arms and legs as they prepared to fight, and said that

dreaded word 'wrestlers' to themselves, and then hurried indoors, desperate to make sure they didn't get into trouble.

'You'd better get started,' said Robin. 'We need to get those armed guards away from that tower, so Milo and Jack can get in.'

'Good,' nodded Big Rock, and he shuffled towards Sam, then reached out and put his big hand on his shoulder.

Immediately, Sam grabbed Big Rock by the wrist and threw him over his shoulder, to crash into the cobbles.

Big Rock pushed himself to his feet, and shook his head. Then he smiled. 'Good wrestling,' he beamed.

Chapter 5

Milo and Jack watched from the cover of an alleyway as the soldiers continued marching backwards and forwards in front of the entrance to the tower. Milo strained his ears for any sounds of shouting or commotion from the direction of the town square.

'Maybe Big Rock and Sam haven't started wrestling yet,' he murmured.

'Or maybe everyone's too scared to go out and watch them,' suggested Jack.

Milo nodded. 'I think you might be right,' he said. He took a deep breath. 'So it's up to us!'

'You mean we're going to go over there and attack those soldiers?' said Jack, horrified.

'Don't be silly!' said Milo. 'We're going to sneak to them!'

Milo left the cover of the alleyway and ran over towards the entrance to the tower, Jack close on his heels. Immediately, the soldiers turned towards them, the points of their spears aimed at their chests.

'Halt!' cried one. 'Who goes there?'

'There's wrestling going on!' yelled Milo, and he pointed towards the town square. 'Two big men! Actually wrestling! In broad daylight, and in public!'

'Wrestling!' said one of the soldiers, shocked. Immediately, he turned to the others. 'You four, come with me!' He pointed at the remaining soldier. 'You, stay here on guard.'

'Yes, sir!' said the soldier.

The five soldiers ran off towards the town square, and the soldier left behind leapt smartly to attention. Jack noticed a big bunch of keys hanging from the soldier's belt, and gestured towards them to Milo. Milo nodded, then turned to the soldier.

'A terrible thing, wrestling,' he said.

'A crime!' agreed the soldier.

'All those tricky moves,' nodded Milo. 'Especially in tag wrestling. Have you ever seen tag wrestling?'

'Wrestling is a crime!' snapped the soldier. 'Watching wrestling is a crime!'

'I know,' nodded Milo. 'Especially tag wrestling. It's one of the biggest crimes there is. It's when two wrestlers are in the same team, and they work together. Like, say, one of them drops to his hands and knees behind an opponent.'

As Milo said this, Jack dropped to his hands and knees immediately behind the soldier.

'And then the other one pushes the opponent.'

And, as Milo said this, he pushed the soldier, who was so startled he didn't have time to recover and fell backwards over the kneeling Jack and landed flat on his back on the ground. Immediately, Milo hurled himself onto the soldier, holding him down on the ground in a pinfall.

'Grab his keys!' yelled Milo.

Jack snatched the keys from the guard's belt and ran up the stone stairs as fast as he could, heading for the prison cell at the top of the tower. Behind him, he could hear the soldier shouting and thrashing about, but Milo was holding him firmly down.

Jack reached the top landing of the tower and found one door there. He fumbled with the keys, trying different ones that didn't fit the lock, all the time urging himself to go quicker. Milo wouldn't be able to hold the soldier for long, he knew, and then he'd raise the alarm!

At last he found a key that worked! He turned the key, opened the cell door, and ran in.

'Princess!' he called.

The next second he felt a powerful thud in his back, which sent him hurtling forwards to fall face first on the hard stone floor. As he lay there, dazed, he heard the sound of running footsteps, and then pain as someone jumped on his back. He was being attacked! There must have been a guard inside the cell.

As Jack heard pounding footsteps rushing towards him again, he rolled over and at the same time swung his right leg, catching his attacker on the shin.

His attacker fell, sprawling. Jack leapt to his feet and went into a wrestling stance, hands in front of him, knees bent ready to deal with the next move.

His attacker sprang up from the floor of the cell, but – to Jack's astonishment – it wasn't a guard, but the small, thin figure of Princess Ava herself. Jack's mouth dropped open, and he moved towards her.

'Princess –' he began.

That was as far as he got. The Princess took a leap towards him, then sprang into the air and kicked out with both her feet in a hard drop kick that struck Jack fully in the chest, sending him staggering backwards. Before Jack could recover, the Princess was on him, grabbing his left wrist and rolling backwards, sending Jack soaring up into the air, then over her head to crash onto the hard floor of the cell.

'No assassin can beat me!' yelled the Princess.

'I'm not –' began Jack, but once again the Princess moved like lightning, this time dropping on Jack with both knees.

'Ow!' said Jack.

A commotion just outside the cell made Jack and the Princess look towards the doorway, just as four armed soldiers rushed in. Milo was being held by two of them. The other two soldiers pointed their spears at Jack and the Princess.

'Stop!' shouted one of them. 'Put your hands up! Move back to the wall!'

Slowly, Jack and the Princess got to their feet and moved towards the wall, their hands held above their heads. Jack's ribs ached from where the Princess's knees had hit him.

The two soldiers holding Milo pushed him towards Jack and the Princess.

'Right,' said the leading soldier. 'You three will stay here until General Pepper decides what to do with you.'

With that, the soldiers backed out of the cell,

and pulled the door shut. Jack heard the key turn in the lock.

'Where were you?' demanded Milo angrily. 'I held the guard down as long as I could, but then those others turned up!'

'She attacked me,' said Jack, pointing an accusing finger at Princess Ava.

The small red-headed girl stood and scowled at the two boys. Seeing her in her long blue dress embroidered with gold and silver threads, it was hard for Jack to think that she was the same fiery wrestler who'd just floored him.

'Attacked you?' echoed Milo, puzzled. He turned to the Princess. 'Why, when we came here to rescue you?'

'I didn't know that!' responded Princess Ava heatedly. 'I've been expecting General Pepper to send an assassin to kill me, so I thought that's who you were.'

Milo turned to Jack.

'But even so, you should have been able to drag her out. She's just a girl.'

'No, she's not,' said Jack ruefully, and he

rubbed his ribs. 'She's a wrestler.'

'A what?'

'I'm a wrestler,' said Princess Ava defiantly. 'And I'd be a good one, too, if I was allowed to wrestle. But I can't because I'm a Princess.' Suddenly she looked very miserable. 'And there's even less chance of me being a wrestler while I'm locked up in here! Or if I'm assassinated!'

'That won't happen!' Milo assured her.

'Why?' demanded the Princess.

'Because . . .' began Milo. Then he stopped.

'Because you're here to rescue me?' the Princess finished for him, sarcastically. 'Well that plan's a bust!'

'Not just us,' said Jack. 'There are more of us!'

'Oh?' said the Princess, brightening. 'Has the resistance movement risen up? How many are there? Hundreds? Thousands?'

'Er . . . two,' said Jack. 'Three, if you count the horse.'

'Two?!'

'Yes, but two very powerful characters,' said Milo. 'Both wrestlers! Big Rock, a Wrestling Troll and Sam Dent! They won't let themselves get caught so easily!'

The sound of the key in the lock made them turn towards the cell door just as it opened and a soldier looked in. He gave them a nasty grin.

'Just thought I'd let you know, your two wrestling pals have been arrested and locked up in the town jail. Oh, and General Pepper says you two are to be executed for treason, for trying to rescue the Princess!'

With that, the cell door was slammed shut, and they heard the key turn in the lock again.

Chapter 6

Big Rock and Sam sat on the stone benches in the town jail. Both looked gloomy.

'No uprising,' sighed Big Rock. 'No people help us.'

Sam gave an even bigger sigh. 'I suppose they were all just too scared,' he admitted. Then he brightened up. 'But if Milo and Jack have been able to free the Princess, then the people will rally round, I'm sure!'

They heard a voice calling, 'Hey!' from outside. It was Robin.

Big Rock and Sam went to the window of the cell and looked out through the iron bars. The old horse was standing there.

'Any news?' asked Sam eagerly. 'Did Milo

and Jack rescue Princess Ava?'

'No,' said Robin. 'They ended up being locked in the tower with her. And they're going to be executed for treason.'

Big Rock let out a groan that was so loud it made the bricks of the walls rattle.

'Can you two break out of there?' asked Robin.

'No,' said Sam. He gripped the iron bars of the cell. 'These bars are set too deep into the wall. We've tried pushing against them but we can't get enough leverage.'

Robin looked at the iron bars of the window thoughtfully. Then he said, 'Wait there,' and trotted off.

Sam sighed. 'Wait there,' he echoed. 'Where does he think we're going to go?'

Inside the room at the top of the tower, Milo paced, his brain working frantically as he tried to come up with a plan to get them out of this spot. Jack sat on the floor and looked at Princess Ava, sitting on the one chair in the room, her face deep in a thoughtful frown.

'I don't understand this,' said Jack. 'We saw you just a week ago at Lord Veto's. You were the special VIP guest at the Orcs versus Trolls Slamdown.'

'And it was when I came back from there that I found my uncle had taken over. He took the opportunity of my being away to declare himself ruler of Weevil, and had me arrested as soon as I got back.'

'Yes, that's what Sam Dent told us,' said Jack. 'But I can't understand how it can all have happened so quickly! In just a week!'

'Fear,' said Milo. 'There's nothing like a load of heavily armed soldiers knocking on doors to frighten people.' He looked hopefully at Jack. 'Maybe if I kicked you, it would make you angry and you'd turn into Thud?' he suggested.

'It didn't work when she kicked me,' said Jack unhappily. 'Or when she threw me over her shoulder.' He turned to Princess Ava and said, 'You are a very good wrestler.'

'I know I am but, let's face it, you're rubbish,' said Princess Ava. 'You couldn't wrestle your way out of a paper bag!'

'That's not fair!' protested Jack. 'You caught me off guard!'

'Well that's one of the things a wrestler has to do,' said Princess Ava. 'Make sure they're not caught off guard.'

There was the sound of a key turning in the lock, and Princess Ava sprang to her feet, ready to attack. The sight of two soldiers pointing their sharp spears at her made her stop.

'If you had the guts to put those weapons down and face me unarmed, I'd show you who's boss!' snapped the Princess angrily.

A short man walked into the cell, dressed in fine clothes embroidered with gold decorations, and with a gold chain hanging around his neck. He had a nasty smile on his face. This had to be General Pepper, realised Jack.

'And if I were stupid, I would let them put their weapons down,' smirked General Pepper. 'But, as it is, I'm not stupid, and I'm also the boss.'

'Nor for long!' growled Princess Ava. 'I am the royal Princess, you are just a general –'

'I'm also your uncle, which means I have royal blood too,' snapped General Pepper. 'Therefore I have the right to be King.'

'You can't be king while I'm alive!' countered the Princess. 'As soon as I reach the age of fifteen, in two month's time, I shall become Queen!'

'Providing you are still alive then,' said General Pepper. Once more he smiled his nasty smile. 'Which, I have to tell you, looks highly unlikely. Once your two friends here have been executed, you will also be executed for treason.'

'You can't execute the Princess!' said Jack, horrified.

'Oh yes I can,' said General Pepper. 'In fact, I've set the date for all your executions as tomorrow. That should stop anyone else from thinking they can rise up in revolution.' He smiled again. 'We'll be doing it in the old-fashioned way: public beheadings in the town square. I do like to keep up the old traditions.'

With that, General Pepper turned and swept out. The two soldiers scowled at Milo, Jack and the Princess and followed General Pepper out of the room, and then the three prisoners heard the key turn in the lock once more.

Chapter 7

Inside their cell, Big Rock and Sam were feeling gloomier than ever.

'I can't see what a horse can do,' groaned Sam.

A whinnying noise outside in the street made them get up.

'That sound like Robin,' said Big Rock.

They both went to the cell window and looked out through the bars. Robin was standing just outside, a long length of chain in his mouth.

'What?' asked Big Rock.

Once more, Robin made a whinnying sound.

'I think he wants us to take the chain from him,' said Sam.

Sam reached through the bars, took hold of

the chain and pulled it into the cell. They now saw that the other end of the length of chain was hooked over Robin's bridle.

'Thank you,' said Robin.

'Why you make that whinny noise?' asked Big Rock, puzzled. 'Why not use proper words like you usually do?'

'Because it's very hard to speak when you've got a mouthful of chain,' said Robin impatiently. 'Right, tie the chain round the bars.'

Sam looped the end of the chain round the bars, and then tied it in a tight knot.

'Ready?' asked Robin.

'Ready,' nodded Sam.

Robin turned away from the window and began to run as fast as his old legs could carry him. Suddenly he jerked to a stop as the chain pulled him up short.

'It's not going to work!' said Sam despairingly.

'Shut up!' said Robin tersely. 'I know what I'm doing.'

With that, the horse leaned, pulling the length of chain so that it stretched tight . . . and then

Robin continued to lean, pulling against the chain. Sam and Big Rock heard the bars set into the wall groan and creak as the knotted chain pulled against them. Robin leaned harder, straining and pulling. Gradually the bars began to bend, and then the next second they hurtled out of the cell window in a shower of stones and dried cement, flying through the air to land on the cobbled street outside.

'Right!' said Robin. 'Now to put the next stage of the plan into operation!'

In the tower, Princess Ava watched, frowning, as once again Milo asked Jack how he felt: if there was any sign of misting over his eyes, or a tingling sensation.

'Why are you asking him all these questions?' she demanded. 'Is he ill?' Then, with a note of alarm, she asked: 'Is it catching? Am I going to catch something off him? I don't want to catch a cold! I'm a Princess!'

'No, nothing like that,' Milo assured her hastily. 'It's –'

'It's private,' interrupted Jack firmly, with a warning look at Milo.

Milo hesitated, then he nodded. 'Yes,' he said. 'It's private.'

Princess Ava looked at Jack in horror.

'You mean it's one of those embarrassing illnesses?!' she said. She gave a shudder of disgust. 'Yuk!'

'No, it's nothing like that!' retorted Jack hotly.

'It's –'

'He turns into a troll,' said Milo. 'When he gets angry.'

'It only happened once!' retorted Jack, annoyed.

He turned to Princess Ava and found her staring at him, her mouth open and an expression of shock on her face.

'It's not my fault!' he said defensively. 'And, as far as I know, it's not catching!'

'How old are you?' she asked.

'Why?' asked Jack.

'Because it might be important,' she said.

Jack shrugged. 'I'm ten.' He shrugged. 'But I don't see –'

'When was your birthday?'

'Two weeks ago,' said Jack.

Princess Ava gave a smug smile. 'You're a half-troll!' she announced.

Jack and Milo exchanged puzzled looks. Then they both asked: 'What?'

'A half-troll,' said Princess Ava. 'People who are half-human, half-troll. It usually doesn't show itself until they're about ten years old. My father told me about them. He'd come across one or two on his travels. They're very rare.' She smiled at Jack. 'You should be proud. Half-trolls make fantastic wrestlers!' Then she looked at Jack doubtfully and added: 'Mind, that might not be the case with you. You look a bit weedy. And you were useless when I fought you.'

'Yes, but when he's Thud he's fantastic!'

The Princess frowned. 'Thud?' she said.

'That's what we call him when he turns into a troll.'

'It's only happened once!' snapped Jack angrily.

But before Jack could say any more, they heard the cell door being unlocked, and then Captain Oz marched into the room, accompanied by about a dozen armed soldiers.

'Prisoners!' he barked at them. 'I have orders to take you at once to the town square, where you will be executed.'

Milo, Jack and Princess Ava stared at Captain Oz in shock.

'Hang on a minute!' said Milo, horrified. 'General Pepper said we're to be executed tomorrow! Not today!'

'General Pepper's changed his mind,' said Captain Oz. Turning to one of the soldiers, he ordered: 'Put the chains on them.'

Chapter 8

Big Rock, Sam and Robin stood in the cover of an alley, by the deserted former wrestling hall, and looked out at the town square. A large crowd of townsfolk had assembled, all of them obviously very anxious, and Sam noticed they kept casting worried looks at the armed soldiers around them.

In the centre of the town square was a large wooden chopping block, and standing next to it was a tall muscular man wearing a black hood and holding a large axe, and a smaller man dressed in heavily decorated clothes and wearing a gold chain.

Suddenly there was a commotion at one side of the square and as Sam, Big Rock and Robin watched, they saw a party of soldiers push their way through the crowd. With the soldiers came Milo, Jack and Princess Ava, all of them with chains wrapped around them, pinning their arms to their sides. They came to a stop by the executioner and General Pepper.

'You said this would happen tomorrow!' said Milo accusingly.

'That was before I got word of your friends escaping,' said General Pepper.

'Escaping?' asked Jack.

'Yes. It seems they broke out of the jail. With two dangerous people like that on the loose, I can't afford to take the risk they might come back with more of their kind and try to free you. This way, they won't have time to put together an army.'

'We don't have an army!' protested Milo. 'There's just us! We're harmless!'

'That,' spat General Pepper, 'is what they all say!' He turned to Captain Oz. 'Execute them. Start with him.' General Pepper pointed a finger at Jack.

'But we're innocent!' protested Jack as the soldiers grabbed hold of him and pushed him towards the execution block. 'We haven't done anything wrong!'

'You've broken the law!' snapped General Pepper. 'And for that you shall be punished!'

Sam, Big Rock and Robin tensed as they watched Jack being forced to his knees and his

head placed on the wooden execution block.

'What are we going to do?' asked Sam desperately.

'We go out there and punch people,' said Big Rock. And he moved out of the alleyway to the back of the crowd.

'It doesn't sound much of a plan,' said Sam.

'You got a better idea?' asked Robin.

'No,' admitted Sam. 'It's just that I don't think we're going to get near enough to stop it before that executioner starts swinging his axe.'

Even as he said it, they saw the executioner lifting his axe into the air, the sunlight glinting on the sharp blade. The soldiers were holding Jack down firmly so that he couldn't move.

'Let's go,' said Robin, and he moved out of the alley, gathering speed as he followed Big Rock at the back of the crowd.

'Here we go!' muttered Sam, and he ran after the horse.

'Leave him alone!' yelled Princess Ava, and she struggled frantically, trying to break free from the soldiers who were holding her, but with their fierce grip and the weight of the chains on her, escape was impossible.

Bent over the execution block, Jack gritted his teeth, ready for the axe to fall.

I won't let them see I'm scared! he vowed to himself. Even though I am! I'm not going to cry!

But even as he thought it, his eyes began to fill up with tears. No, not with tears, with a sort of . . . mist. Like thick opaque crystals forming. And, at the same time, he felt a shuddering sensation course through him.

The executioner had his axe raised to the highest point and was just about to bring it down hard on the boy when he realised that something was happening in front of him. The boy was getting up. No, not getting up, he was growing . . . and changing . . . and getting up.

As the executioner watched, goggle-eyed, a huge creature stood up from where the boy had been kneeling. The two soldiers who'd been holding the boy down were now dangling off the creature, their feet kicking the air. The chains around what had been the boy bulged and stretched, and then snapped and broke as the creature became even wider and taller.

'Yes!' yelled Milo exultantly. 'Thud is here!!'

'Wow!' said Princess Ava, awed.

General Pepper stared upwards at the towering figure of Thud, his mouth open, stunned. Then he snapped out of his shock and yelled out, 'Kill it! Kill the troll! Kill all

of them!'

The executioner also came out of his state of shock and began to swing the axe towards Thud, but the huge creature grabbed hold of the axe by the handle and tore it from the executioner's grasp.

Thud gave a snarl and slammed the axe down hard onto the wooden block, smashing both the axe and the block. Then he reached out and grabbed hold of the shocked Captain Oz, lifted him clear off the ground, and threw him into a group of shocked soldiers, knocking them all down.

'Get us out of these chains!' yelled Princess Ava, as she kicked out at the soldiers nearest to her.

'Happy to oblige!' said a voice.

Milo and Ava turned and saw Sam appear beside them. They looked out into the crowd and saw there was even greater commotion going on as Big Rock grabbed the soldiers nearest to him, and other soldiers dropped to the ground as Robin charged into them.

'Long live Princess Ava!' came a sudden shout from the crowd. And then they heard other voices taking the call up so that it became a chant: 'Princess Ava! Princess Ava!'

Milo became aware that some of the crowd had now also turned on the soldiers. Desperately, the soldiers tried to defend themselves, but as their spears and swords were snatched away from them, many of the soldiers turned and ran.

Meanwhile, Thud was causing havoc, picking up the terrified soldiers and slamming them down on the ground where they lay stunned and senseless.

'Where's General Pepper?' called Milo, searching the crowds, but Pepper seemed to have vanished, lost in the masses. Then suddenly Milo saw him, plucked out of the crowd and held aloft in one of Big Rock's huge fists.

'Here he is!' called Big Rock.

The troll whirled General Pepper around his head, then released him to sail through the air. Thud reached up and skilfully caught the horrified General Pepper, turned him upside down, slammed him to the ground and then fell on him, pinning him down.

'Tag wrestling!' grinned Milo. 'I love it!'

Chapter 9

Within minutes it was all over. General Pepper and Captain Oz were sprawled on the ground, chained together, both looking dazed and bruised. The soldiers who hadn't thrown away their weapons and run were now also sitting on the ground in chains, prisoners.

Big Rock had lifted the Princess up and placed her on his shoulders, so she could acknowledge the crowd as they cheered her and chanted her name. Milo and Jack stood to one side, next to Robin, and joined in the applause for the Princess.

'I still don't know why it happens,' whispered Jack, once again a small, thin boy.

'Just be thankful it did,' whispered back Milo.

Then, with Ava still riding on Big Rock's shoulders, and Sam leading the cheering crowd, they escorted the Princess through the town to the royal palace. Milo, Jack and Robin brought up the end of the procession, just behind General Pepper and Captain Oz and the captured soldiers, who were all loaded down with chains and looking very miserable.

It took another hour for the procession to

reach the palace because so many of the crowd wanted to shake Princess Ava's hand, or bow to her. All of them were also eager to shake the hands of Milo, Big Rock, Sam and Jack . . . although it was obvious that mostly they were very nervous and wary of getting too close to Jack.

When they at last reached the royal palace, Milo noticed that nearly everyone gave Robin an affectionate pat just before they left to go back to their homes.

'Idiots!' grumbled Robin half under his breath, but Milo was sure that the old horse was secretly pleased with the attention he was getting.

Big Rock put the Princess down, and she swept majestically in through the doors of the palace, followed by Sam Dent, Big Rock, the captives, and Milo, Jack and Robin. Once the doors had shut, she turned to her rescuers and said with a sigh of relief, 'I'm glad that's over!'

'What are we going to do with this lot?' asked Milo, gesturing at General Pepper and Captain Oz, and the unhappy chained-up soldiers.

'They're too dangerous to be left walking around free,' added Sam.

'I'm not dangerous!' called out Captain Oz. 'I pledge my allegiance to Princess Ava!'

General Pepper turned and glared at the Captain. 'Traitor!' he spat at him.

'I shall send a messenger to my cousin Edward,' Princess Ava decided. 'He's king of the next kingdom. He never liked Uncle Pepper; he always warned me about him as being sneaky and treacherous.' She looked at the scowling General Pepper. 'I'm sure that King Edward will be pleased to come and take these traitors away and put them in prison, and make them work hard!' She turned to Big Rock and said, 'Will you take them downstairs for me, Big Rock? There's a very damp dungeon down there. They can wait there until King Edward sends his people to collect them.'

'Good,' said Big Rock. And he ushered the chained-up villains towards the stone steps and the dungeons below.

The Princess turned to Jack. 'Also, I take back

what I said before about you being rubbish! You are awesome when you're . . . the wrestling you.'

'Thud,' said Milo. 'His name is Thud.'

'Jack,' corrected Jack. 'My name is Jack.'

'Well, Jack Thud, it was brilliant to see you in action. I owe you my life.' She turned to Milo, Sam and Robin. 'I owe my life to all of you! And I won't forget it.'

Big Rock returned.

'Bad people locked in dungeon,' he announced.

'Good,' said Princess Ava. 'And now, I'd like you all to follow me.'

Chapter 10

As Princess Ava headed towards the grand staircase and began to go up it, Jack and Milo gave each other puzzled looks.

'What's going on?' whispered Jack.

'No idea,' said Milo. He turned to Sam who shrugged, equally puzzled.

They followed the Princess up the stairs to the landing, and joined her by a door she had just opened.

'There!' she said proudly.

They walked into the room, then all stopped and stared, stunned.

The room was the biggest Jack had ever seen – even bigger than the largest rooms in Veto Castle. It looked like a ballroom, except for the rows of seats around all four of the walls, facing inwards. And, there, in the very centre of the huge room . . .

'It's a wrestling ring!' breathed Milo, awed.

And it certainly was – one of the most beautifully decorated and ornate wrestling rings that any of the gang had ever seen.

'My father had it built,' said Princess Ava. 'He liked to invite special wrestlers to come to the palace for private bouts.'

'Wow!' said Milo, still awestruck by the sight of the magnificent ring in the middle of the huge room.

'It's wonderful,' said Jack.

'Good place to wrestle,' nodded Big Rock.

'So would you, Big Rock?' asked the Princess.

'Love to,' he nodded.

'Against me,' added the Princess shyly.

They all looked at her in surprise.

'You?' said Milo.

'The thing is, I've always wanted to be a wrestler. But, because I'm a Princess, I'm not allowed to. But it's always been my dream that one day I'd be in the ring with a professional wrestler. And to be in there with a great Wrestling Troll like Big Rock would be the best thing ever!'

'You're certainly good enough,' Jack told her. 'You beat me.'

Big Rock lumbered towards the ring, and the Princess gave a shout of delight and ran towards it herself.

Sam stopped Big Rock and whispered warningly: 'If you hurt her, you'll have me to deal with.'

Big Rock smiled. 'Fun only,' he said. 'No one get hurt.'

'I wouldn't be so sure of that,' muttered Jack. 'You'd better watch yourself, Big Rock. She's got a powerful kick on her.'

Jack and Milo took their seats at the ringside as Big Rock and the Princess climbed through the ropes into the ring. Robin sat down on the floor beside them.

Big Rock and the Princess circled each other. Suddenly the Princess leapt up into the air, aiming herself at Big Rock, and did a drop kick. Both her feet slammed hard against the troll's chest before she landed back on the canvas and did an elegant roll and somersault to take her away from Big Rock, in case he fell and landed on her.

'If that had been anyone else but Big Rock, that would have hurt!' murmured Jack.

'She's good,' nodded Milo in agreement.

Even though he was a hard-as-stone troll, the Princess's dropkick had sent Big Rock stumbling backwards a few paces. Now Big Rock went into a crouch, his huge hands and arms out in front of him, ready to fend off the next attack.

This time, the Princess waited in the centre of the ring, crouching low herself, her arms and hands out in front of her. Suddenly Big Rock made his move, running fast towards her with a speed that was surprising in someone whose bulk was so huge, and for one awful moment Jack thought that the Princess was going to be crushed. Instead, as Big Rock reached her, the Princess ducked beneath Big Rock's arms, grabbed his huge thighs with her small hands, and suddenly straightened up. The next second Big Rock was sailing forwards over her head and crashing down behind her.

'A Back Body Drop!' said Jack, awed. 'She did a Back Body Drop on Big Rock!'

Big Rock and the Princess carried on trading moves and holds and throws. The two had been in the ring for about five minutes, each giving the other as good as they could, when the Princess suddenly ran towards Big Rock, jumped up, put one foot on one of his rocky knees, and then leapt up so that she had her arms around his head. She then threw herself backwards, her arms still around Big Rock's head, dragging the troll forwards at speed. As the Princess landed on the mat in a sitting position, she still held onto Big Rock's head, and he hit the canvas with his face.

'A Bulldog!' grinned Jack.

As Big Rock lay on the canvas, Princess Ava suddenly gave a huge heave with her feet and arms, rolled the big troll onto his back, and then leapt on him, pinning his shoulders to the canvas.

'One! Two! Three!' counted Sam.

The Princess rolled off the troll and sprang to her feet. Sam grabbed her hand and held it aloft. 'I declare the winner to be: Princess Ava!'

Milo and Jack applauded and cheered. As Big Rock got to his feet, the Princess scowled at him. 'You let me win,' she said accusingly.

'Yes,' agreed Big Rock. 'It only fair. Me troll. You human. But you good wrestler.'

'Yes you are,' said Milo as he came to the ring with Jack. 'It's a pity you can't go into the ring and let everyone see how good you are.'

'I wish I could,' said the Princess sadly, 'but it wouldn't fit with me being Queen.' Then she said thoughtfully: 'But perhaps, sometimes, I could take a trip to another country where a wrestling tournament's going on, and where my friends are part of the bill. And maybe I could join them.'

'People would recognise you,' said Jack. 'Word would get back to Weevil.'

'Not if she wore a mask,' said Robin.

Everyone turned to look at the old horse in stunned awe.

'That is a brilliant idea!' said Sam.

Princess Ava smiled. 'Yes!' she said. 'I could be the Masked Avenger! And the only way anyone could get to take my mask off was if they beat me in a match!'

'The Masked Avenger!' smiled Big Rock, impressed. 'Brilliant!'

'Until then, I've got to be a Princess and get my country back together again,' said Ava. 'One of the first things I'll be doing is passing a law allowing wrestling back! And, to organise that,

I appoint Sam Dent, the greatest wrestler ever to come from this kingdom.' She turned to Sam and said, 'You'd better kneel.'

'Why?' asked Sam, puzzled.

'Because it's traditional when giving out a knighthood.'

Sam stared at her, stunned. Then a smile spread over his face. 'Wrestlers don't kneel,' he said. 'Not unless they lose a contest.'

With the same speed and swiftness she'd

shown in the ring with Big Rock, Princess Ava dropped and swung out a leg, catching Sam just below the knee and making him fall. Then just as quickly, she bounced back to her feet as Sam was about to push himself up, but instead he found himself caught in a headlock by the Princess and forced back down to his knees.

'Submit?' she asked.

'I kneel,' grinned Sam.

Princess Ava released her grip from around his head and stepped back. 'Arise, Sir Sam Dent,' she said.

Sam got up, and forced a rueful grin at Big Rock, Milo, Jack and Robin.

'I could have taken her,' he said defensively. 'But she is my future Queen.'

'Oh yes, like we believe you!' said Robin, rolling his eyes.

Chapter 11

The old caravan moved slowly along the country road, heading away from the small town of Weevil. As before, Milo and Jack sat in the driving seat. Once again, Big Rock, the Wrestling Troll, ran around the caravan, all the time throwing punches at the empty air.

'We go back soon?' he asked.

'Soon-ish,' nodded Milo. 'We need to give Princess Ava and Sam time to get the wrestling up and running properly again.'

'Sir Sam,' corrected Jack.

Milo grinned. 'Sir Sam,' he said.

'Ridiculous!' snorted Robin. 'Whoever heard of a wrestler getting a knighthood? Next thing, they'll be giving them out to people like . . .

well, actors and singers.' He snorted again. 'Ridiculous!'

'Anyway, thanks to Princess Ava, at least I know why I turn into Thud,' said Jack. He shook his head. 'I'm a half-troll, and I never knew it!'

'Did she mention anything about how to control it?' asked Milo.

'No,' said Jack. 'She just said that's one of the problems with being a half-troll: learning to control it. She said if I can, it would be fantastic.'

'It certainly would,' said Milo. 'Being able to turn into a troll when you want to, not when your inner troll takes over when you get angry or upset. Now that would be brilliant for wrestling!'

'Yes,' sighed Jack. 'But how do I learn to control it?'

'That's what we've got to find out,' said Milo. 'And we will!'

Suddenly Jack and Milo were aware of a curious sound, low at first, but now getting stronger, almost melodic. And then Jack realised what it was. Robin was singing!

Jack looked at Milo and grinned. And then both joined in with the old horse as he plodded along, hauling the caravan. And soon Big Rock had joined in as well, and the fields and mountains and rivers echoed to the sound of their song:

'Wrestling Trolls
'Tum-di-dum!
'Wrestling Trolls
'Tum-di-dum!'

Get ready for more adventures with the Wrestling Trolls in

MATCH 2 HUNK and THUD

Jack is doing fantastically well as the Wrestling Trolls training coach, Big Rock is winning matches, and the group are on their way to more gold and tasty rocks than they can count. All Jack has to do is keep his alter-ego THUD! under control...

Read on for a sneak peek of
HUNK and THUD!

The venue for the Riverdam Slam was absolutely packed. Some of the crowd had dressed up as their favourite wrestlers.

There were at least ten people wearing costumes made to look like Big Rock's multi-patched one, with a picture of a mountain top on the front. About six had come dressed as the wrestler Sam Dent; four girls had dressed up as Grit, the new rising girl-troll star; and two people had perched one on top of the other inside a large sack that had 'Ug the Giant' written on it.

There were at least eight people dressed as

Orcs, complete with fake talons and with red eyeshadow painted around their eyes.

One person was wearing a full-face hood in honour of the Masked Avenger. No one was dressed as Hunk, but Jack guessed that was because Hunk the Half-Troll was a new face on the scene, and no one knew enough about him yet.

The hall lights began to dim, and the harsh bright lights above the ring came on. Into the ring stepped the Master of Ceremonies, wearing a brightly coloured waistcoat and a big yellow bow tie.

'My lords, ladies and gentlemen!' he boomed, his voice filling the hall. 'Welcome to the fantastic Riverdam Slam, featuring some of the greatest wrestlers on the scene today, as well as introducing some of the newest and up and coming wrestling stars of the future!'

At this, the crowd erupted into cheers and stamped their feet and whistled, subsiding as the Master of Ceremonies waved his hands to ask for quiet.

As an expectant hush settled over the crowd, the Master of Ceremonies once again beamed at them and made his announcement, but this time his voice had an apologetic tone.

'Today's programme was due to begin with a contest between Hunk the Half-Troll and Ug the Giant,' he announced. 'But, unfortunately, Ug was taken ill with stomach ache not long ago, and he's had to withdraw.'

'Stomach ache?' queried Milo, puzzled over the news about Ug. 'That's unusual. Most of the giants I've met could eat anything without suffering stomach ache.'

Jack looked around and saw Hunk standing at the back of another section of the hall, his attention fully on the ring in the middle of the hall. If he was disappointed at not being able to take part in the event, he didn't look it.

The crowd shouted out its disappointment, but before things could get out of hand the Master of Ceremonies flashed a big smile and boomed into the microphone, drowning out any unhappy noises. 'So instead we move to the next bout on the bill. A brilliant young rising star of Troll Wrestling, the truly formidable, and so far unbeaten . . . my lords, ladies and gentlemen, I give you . . . Grit!'

With that, the curtain at the back of the hall opened and the small, stocky figure of Grit appeared. Her wrestling costume of brightly multi-coloured spangles twinkled and shone, matching the crystalline of her rocky and stony skin.

Grit waved at the crowd, who cheered the small troll loudly as she stomped down the aisle to the ring, and pulled herself into it through the ropes.

While Grit stood in one corner of the ring and waited, the MC took centre stage again.

'And now, Grit's opponent, that mystery wrestler who is known only as the Masked Avenger! Yes, ladies and gentlemen, she wears a mask to hide her identity. Who is she? There will be only ever be one way for her mask to come off and her identity to be known. If she loses, then the person who defeats her has the right to take the mask from her head! Will that be her fate today against Grit?'

At this, there rose a huge cheer from the crowd, along with shouts of, 'Yes!' and 'Take her mask off! Take her mask off!'

'My lords, ladies and gentlemen!' boomed the MC, flinging his arm towards the curtains at the back of the hall. 'Let's have a huge Riverdam Slam welcome for . . . the Masked Avenger!'

The curtains parted and into the hall stepped Jack and Milo's friend, Princess Ava, dressed as the Masked Avenger. Her costume was purple and she wore a hood with two eyeholes in it completely covering her head. The crowd continued chanting, 'Take her mask off! Take her mask off!' as Princess Ava ran down the aisle, somersaulted over the ropes into the ring to land nimbly on her feet, and then did another somersault into the centre of the ring.

It was strange for Jack to see two wrestlers he liked battling each other – but he would always have to root for his friend Princess Ava.

He didn't want her identity to be revealed, ever!

The Masked Avenger saluted the crowd as the MC announced, 'The rules: the first to get two pinfalls or two submissions to a count of three, or a knockout to a count of ten, is the winner. And now, let the action begin!'

The bell by the side of the ring sounded.

The Riverdam Slam was underway!

The Masked Avenger darted out of her corner and threw herself at Grit, her short, stocky girl-troll opponent. Jack winced and half-closed his eyes in anticipation of the Avenger crashing into the solid, rocky figure. Instead the Avenger surprised everyone, including Grit, by suddenly dropping to the canvas seconds before she hit Grit and sliding into the small troll's shins. She grabbed the troll's legs with both hands, and then slid around behind her, pulling back to try and pull the troll over.

It didn't work.

Grit used her weight and her low centre of gravity to remain solidly upright. Then she reached down, grabbed the Avenger by one arm and threw her up into the air, caught her as she came down, and hurled her hard at the nearest corner post.

The Masked Avenger thudded into the post and crashed to the canvas.

'Ouch!' winced Jack. 'That must have hurt.'

'I told you Grit was good,' murmured Milo.

Grit lurched towards the corner, one foot raised to crunch the Avenger beneath it, but the Avenger rolled swiftly away, and Grit's foot stamped down on the canvas, narrowly missing the Avenger.

The Avenger bounced up and leapt backwards as Grit turned and lunged at her. Once again Grit just missed. The Avenger was fast.

The Avenger went on the attack again, this time jumping high and leaping on to Grit's shoulders, her feet gripping Grit's head on either side. Then the Avenger tried a forward roll, but again Grit used her weight and low centre of gravity to stand still, like a rock. Grit slammed her hands up to clap the Avenger's ankles to the sides of her head, and the Avenger found herself upside down with her feet trapped in Grit's rocky fists.

BANG!

Grit slammed the Avenger down head first and then let go of her ankles.

The Avenger, dazed by the double blow to the top of her head, fell down and immediately Grit fell on her, pinning both the Avenger's shoulders to the canvas. Although she struggled hard to lift first one shoulder, then the other, the Avenger was no match for the troll-type weight of Grit.

'One!' shouted the crowd approvingly, as the referee began the count. 'Two! Three!'

Grit pushed herself up off the fallen Avenger and returned to her corner, while the crowd erupted with shouts of, 'Grit! Grit! Grit!' and 'Take her mask off!'

'It's not looking good for Ava,' said Jack, worried. 'It'll finish her wrestling career if she gets unmasked here.'

Find out what happens to Ava
in the next instalment of

Wrestling Trolls:

**COMING
SOON!**

Don't miss these other exciting adventures from Hot Key Books ...

The Great Galloon is an enormous airship, built by
Captain Meredith Anstruther and manned by his
crew, who might seem like a bit of a motley bunch
but who are able to fight off invading marauders
whilst drinking tea and sweeping floors!

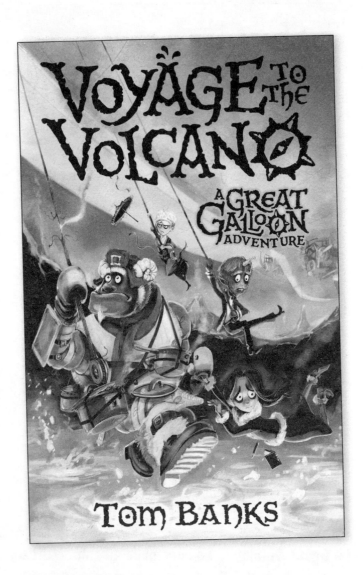

**Captain Anstruther and his motley crew of
sky-pirates are back for more adventures!**

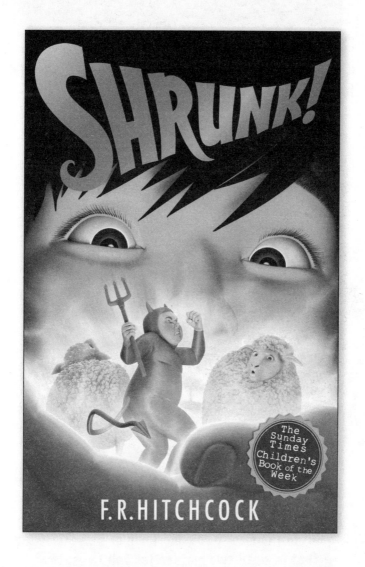

A squirrel, a hot dog stand, the planet Jupiter...
what will get shrunk next?

THE SUNDAY TIMES 'Book of the Week'

All is quiet in the sleepy seaside town of Bywater-by-Sea
- that is, until two meteorites fall to earth -
landing in the middle of the Field Craft Troop's
outdoor expedition camp.

Uniquely written by 2000 children and Fleur Hitchcock
in the online live writing project, TheStoryAdventure.com

THE

TROUBLE
WITH MUMMIES

F. R. HITCHCOCK

Probably the first really noticeable thing was
Mum coming back from the hairdresser's on
Friday afternoon, wearing a small black beard.

HARVEY DREW
AND THE BIN MEN
FROM OUTER SPACE

Harvey Drew is an ordinary eleven-year-old
who dreams of great adventures in outer space.
The Toxic Spew is an intergalactic waste disposal ship.
The two are on a collision course for chaos!

ARCHIE KIMPTON
JUMBLE CAT

ILLUSTRATED BY KATE HINDLEY

Billy Slipper is a fairly normal boy with a definitely
not-so-fairly normal family. All he wants to do is add
to his 'Collectabillya' (an assortment of weird and
wonderful objects he finds) in peace, but his cleaning-
mad mum (she even clingfilms the carrots!) and his
fantastically horrid twin sister have other ideas.